W9-CBT-918

GOOD-BY MY SHADOW

Mary Stolz *is also the author of:*

To Tell Your Love
The Organdy Cupcakes
The Sea Gulls Woke Me
Ready or Not
In a Mirror
Pray Love, Remember
Rosemary
The Day and the Way We Met
Hospital Zone
Because of Madeline

GOOD-BY MY SHADOW

by Mary Stolz

HARPER & BROTHERS
Publishers *New York*

GOOD-BY MY SHADOW

Printed in the United States of America

The poem "Growing Up," by Marchette Chute, on page 181, is from *St. Nicholas Magazine*, copyright, 1935, by Educational Publishing Corporation. Used by permission of the author.

The poem "Grown-up," by Edna St. Vincent Millay, on page 181, is from *Collected Poems*, Harper & Brothers, copyright, 1921, 1949, by Edna St. Vincent Millay. Used by permission.

LIBRARY OF CONGRESS CATALOG CARD NUMBER: 57-9266

To
Mr. Herrick

PART ONE

CHAPTER ONE

On the afternoon of Christmas Eve it began to rain. Barbara Perry, who took everything personally, stood at the dining-room window, filled with reproach, and looked at the dripping garden. It looked so shining, so gray and unspeakably wet. Barbara glared at it, trying with her eyes to force a slackening in the rain, or, better still, convert it to snow. Was there just a touch of white in the falling drops, just a tendency to drift? Was there—she glanced at her watch—still time for the treacherous afternoon to behave itself and so save the evening? Two o'clock. They were to go caroling at eight. Yes, if it would get colder, if this rain would turn to snow, the evening could go forward as planned. But it would have to be done immediately. She leaned toward the window till her nose touched the cold glass and her breath fogged it. In the garden the rain continued to fall.

"It isn't fair," Barbara muttered. "It simply just isn't *fair.*"

"What isn't?" said her mother, who was at the sideboard arranging a centerpiece of French heather, holly, and Christmas balls. The magazine article on flower arrangement had instructed her to be bold, to let her imagination run riot. It had said further that there was no end to the unusual effects to be achieved in this manner. The effect she'd achieved was more untidy than unusual, and Mrs. Perry felt that magazine articles on flower arrangement were probably not intended for women who liked asparagus fern, which she did (though she always threw it out). "What do you think of this?" she asked as her daughter turned away from the window.

"What is that stuff?"

"French heather."

Barbara shook her head. "I don't like it very much. It looks dry, or something."

"I suppose," Mrs. Perry said with resignation, "that some imaginations aren't meant to run riot." She thrust the remaining Christmas balls into the bowl, on top of the holly, put the bowl in the center of the table. "It'll just have to do."

"Oh, well," said Barbara. She really couldn't care. "Mother, I said it was raining."

"Did you, dear?" Mrs. Perry waited. Her glance

strayed to the centerpiece, back to Barbara, who looked pretty and indignant. She really is all eyes, thought her mother. And she has such sense about her appearance. This way of wearing practically no lipstick, so that her eyes show up even more. Barbara knows how to achieve effects. Yes, she was a very pretty girl, who seemed to be in a constant state of discontent, and Mrs. Perry didn't see what there was to do about it. From time to time, during the past couple of years, both she and her husband had tried having talks with Barbara, for her own good. Mrs. Perry knew perfectly well how annoying and generally useless a talk for one's own good was, and yet—if it really *were* for good? She sighed now, but not audibly. Talks had gotten them nowhere, gotten Barbara nowhere. She seemed almost unreachable by either love or logic, and probably the only thing to do was wait. And hope. It was terrible to see a child of yours—to see any child—grown from a quite spontaneous and loving person into one armored with self-concern, and no chink visible.

"Mother," Barbara said now, in the politely patient voice she so often assumed with her parents (as though, Mrs. Perry thought, she were doomed to talk with dimwits and simply bore it as best she could), "I've been telling you it's raining, and you just stand there looking at me as if it didn't matter at all."

"I was thinking about you, if that helps."

Barbara looked briefly uneasy, then said, "The only

thing that'll help is for it either to stop raining or start snowing. Otherwise everything's ruined."

"Oh, well," her mother protested. "Everything?"

"Everything," Barbara said seriously. "How can we go caroling in the rain?"

"You can't."

"And even if it doesn't matter about *us,* I mean all our plans, and all, I'd think you'd be sorry about the money. I mean, after all, we do give the money to the Heart Association, and I should think—"

"Barbara," her mother interrupted. "Stop, dear. You sound—" she cast about for a word "—sound so unconvincing. I know you give the money to the Heart Association, and it's a very nice thing—caroling, helping, donating—all of it. But, darling, it's so foolish to pretend it's the *Heart* Association you're concerned about—" Mrs. Perry broke off. What's the matter with me, she wondered. What difference does it make if she pretends it's a few dollars lost to cardiac cases that's making her furious, and not the jeopardy to her own personal plans? Am I always so honest, heaven forbid? "I'm sorry—" she began, but Barbara had retreated to tremulous hauteur.

"I am the one who is sorry," she said coldly, "for being so *unconvincing,* as you put it. And now, if you'll excuse me, Mother—" She walked away, up the stairs, her mother looking helplessly after her.

Yes, but the worst part of it is, Mrs. Perry thought, that I *do* these things, say these unnecessary things, because of something else. I want her to be happy, to stop being so dissatisfied, and because I don't seem to be able to help at all, I pick on every bit of trivia and all I accomplish is to make her more withdrawn. Only why do I believe that Barbara *knows* this, and just won't admit it? "I get awfully tired," she'd said to her husband once, "of people who go around marveling at science and art and calling things miracles and how in the world did they ever get accomplished, when the real miracle is people themselves and growing up, and how in the world *that* ever gets accomplished is beyond me."

"Depends on what you mean by grown up," he'd said. "There're an awful lot of neurotics in the world."

"There are a great number of reasonably stable and mature people, and if you ask me that's more miraculous than the Acropolis or the split atom. I wonder what their parents were like."

"Whose parents?"

"The parents of the adults who are really grown up."

"Probably much like you," he'd said, and she'd seen that he really meant it.

"You're prejudiced," she'd said ruefully, and really meant that. Now she looked at the stairway, reflected in the buffet mirror, half-wishing Barbara would come down again, and half-relieved to know she wouldn't, not for a while. And when she did, she would not be sulky. It was one of Barbara's very nicest qualities, that she didn't sulk. Barbara had a great many lovely qualities, somehow diffused, in these her middle teens, by the extent of her self-absorption. Well, that would pass. If you remembered your own adolescence (and you could, though you never mentioned it any more to Barbara, who inclined to look either doubtful or embarrassed when you did), you had to admit you'd been pretty self-centered, rather dreamy about the existence of other people, and—now that you thought of it—resentful and a bit suspicious of your own mother's occasional mention of *her* adolescence. In fact, Mrs. Perry said to herself, transferring her gaze from the mirrored stairway to the mirrored centerpiece, now that I'm thinking about all this, I remember just hating the word adolescent. So there. What do I mean, so there? Well, I'm not sure what I mean—but I certainly won't call Barbara an adolescent again. Not to her face, anyway.

She approached the centerpiece and began to disassemble it. An imagination that brought together French heather, Christmas balls, and holly shouldn't be allowed to run riot. It should be led on a leash. Probably, she thought, there'd still be time to go out and buy a poinsettia. She looked at the dining-room clock. Two-thirty. Yes, there'd be time. She looked out the window, saw that the rain was turning to snow, began to mutter rebelliously because she hated snow-driving, then remembered Barbara's large block of interest in the weather and cheered up. Actually, with the Christmas balls and the holly removed, the French heather didn't look too bad. Rather dry, a bit brown perhaps, but not bad, rather wistful and parlorish. She went into the living room, hung the balls on the tree, stuck the holly behind some candles on the mantel, assured herself there were times when it was nicer to be traditional than to be imaginative, and decided to stay home.

Everything works out, she thought. Practically everything—given a little time—works out.

Sometimes she found herself calling her own name in her mind. *Barbara?* Or even whispering it aloud. *Barbara?* Not as if she were saying, "Barbara, are you there?" but as if she questioned the existence of this person, and inquired tentatively, inaudibly (so as not to appear a fool if, after all, there turned out to be no Barbara), and so uncertainly that the Barbara of flesh and blood was immediately strengthened, scornful of such weakness, and often was unaware of the troubled call.

Yet she would do it again, without volition, and did so now as she came into her room and shut the door. *Barbara!* Barbara? she half-sang in her mind, and sat in the little chair upholstered in gold velveteen, not looking for a reply. She wished she were one of those who took things easily, stoically. One who could see the rain ruin everything and say, Too bad, but it can't be helped. Because actually, when you came right down to it, what was ruined by the rain? Their plans to go caroling . . .

the world would go none the lamer for the loss of that Christmas rite. The Heart Association would survive, and the eight of them would spend all of Christmas Eve with their families instead of just part.

And it wasn't that she minded that, either. She loved her family. Her mother, who was pretty and understood more than Barbara was prepared to admit to either of them. Her father, who was marvelous, and that wasn't just her own opinion—practically everyone who knew him said so. Everyone who knew him wasn't around all the time and didn't know how exasperating he could be. Still, he was marvelous. And her two young brothers. Well, they were just beyond comprehension. They never found time heavy on their hands, they always had something to do, to think about, and it was impossible to be in their company without feeling cheered and tender and hopeful for the human race as an institution. But how could you understand people who were never bored, never restless? Barbara, who dreamed a great deal, frequently found time heavy on her hands and heart, regarded her brothers with awe and could not formulate them in her mind.

Oh no, it wasn't that she disliked spending Christmas Eve with her family. It was that she disliked passionately having her plans disturbed. It was more than that, today. She got up and wandered to her bureau, stood looking absently at the young face in the mirror. At no time could she bear to have her plans upset, but tonight's had been

. . . Oh, it would have been so much *fun,* she evaded, then met her own eyes and remembered she had promised that reflected person that they'd be honest with each other. All right, then, tonight's plans had been important beyond fun.

The girl in the mirror stared at her solemnly and solemnly she stared back, looking into the hazel eyes with the thick, well-stenciled brows, studying the oval shape of the face, the glossy brown hair that waved naturally. That's all very well, she said, and you can be glad of it, but look into my *mind.* That's what I'm asking you to do. The girl in the mirror continued to care only about externals, forcing Barbara to turn slightly, so that the slim waist looked even slimmer, and the lovely neck was defined. There was a dress she'd seen the other day . . . a primrose-yellow wool that—

She moved away from the glass, furious with herself, real and reflected. But who, she asked silently, stretching her arms in the air, then bringing them close to herself as though enfolding something, who knows her true self from the reflected? She closed her eyes, and it was not her own arms that held her. A boy's young arms held her and a boy's voice said, "Barbara, I love you . . . love you."

Barbara dropped to the bed, biting her lip. I said, I decided and promised to be honest, for at least a few minutes out of the day, with myself. I said that for a little while, when I was alone, I'd drop the acting and the dreaming and the making up of nice things that don't happen. Well then, *do* it. Forget the boy who has never held you close but may someday . . . someday he may, that boy, be real—he'll *have* to be. I'm Barbara Perry, and I'm pretty, and I'm really a nice person, and it isn't possible that never will a boy say, Barbara, I love you . . . love you. . . . Oh, please . . . what's the matter with you? Can't you stop it, even for a minute, even when you make up your mind that you will, you *will*?

Now look, she told herself. Now, see here. For one minute you are going to say something direct and truthful to yourself and you are not going to let *anything* get in the way. Now . . . She looked at the clock, watched the slender red second hand travel one, two, six, sixteen seconds. When it gets to twelve, she told herself, and watched it go smoothly upward till it stood straight, at noon, at midnight, and she said, "I'm a fake," and the hand moved on and down.

So she was a fake. It wasn't news, it wasn't very interesting, it wasn't even terribly important, probably. Because most people were fakes, more or less, weren't they? Were Richard and Andrew, her brothers, fakes? No—but they weren't really old enough to have started fakiness (a quality Barbara felt had been present in herself for about three years, since her twelfth birthday, say, and growing ever since) and besides Andrew and Richard were not most people. And besides that she'd wandered from the point again, which was to admit to herself that she'd wanted to go caroling tonight because she was impressed by the group she had been asked to go with. *There,* she thought a little limply. That's about as honest as anyone could be required to be. Impressed by them and—all right, go a step further—not even asked by them. Mrs. Howard, who was something or other on the Caroling Association that made up these groups from volunteers at the high school, had suggested her. But they'd accepted the suggestion. Margaret Obemeyer, class president of the tenth grade, president of the Pep Club, secretary of the Drama Society, winner of last year's popularity poll, had phoned and mentioned Mrs. Howard's suggestion and then said, "That all right with you, Barbara?"

Barbara, a little breathless, had said, "Gosh, yes. I mean, sure, that'd be fine. Where'll we meet and all?"

"Let's see. You're out Jeff Irwin's way, aren't you? Suppose I ask Jeff to pick you up, I mean his father, he's picking up some others, and then we're driving to Connie Frost's, we're going to start from there and afterward go back and have cocoa and stuff, so whoever's dropping Jeff off can drop you, too. Okay?"

"Sure . . . sure, that'd be swell, Margaret. I'll . . . I'll be ready. What time is it? I mean, when'll Jeff's father come by?"

"Oh, a little before eight. Well, toodle-oo."

Margaret was gone, leaving Barbara elated, and plagued (as she always was) by the notion that her voice on a phone was shrill. She kept trying to remember to keep it low, unhurried, poised, and every time she hung up it echoed in her hearing as shrill, rushed, and rattled.

I don't know, she thought now, sitting on the edge of her bed, hands in her lap, eyes on the floor. There seems to be so much to correct. She sighed, looked out the window, and jumped to her feet. *Snow!* It wasn't raining any more at all—or anyway practically not at all. It was snowing. She threw up the window, leaned out and tipped her face toward the sky. Big fat flakes fell against her cheeks, her eyes. She looked down on the ground. The snow was slowly, just perceptibly, beginning to cling, to turn the wet to whiteness. The air was cold, wonderfully, mercifully cold. She closed the window and hummed, half-closing her eyes, a smile darting at her lips. Oh, it was wonderful, it was lovely, it was dazzling to be so happy— Suddenly she ran down the stairs, and, finding Andrew at the foot, grabbed him in her arms and hugged him.

Andrew grinned up at her, removed himself gently from this sudden embrace, and said, "Hi, Barby. I'm pretty busy."

"Oh, all right. Go along," she laughed. "Fine thing, though, if you can't stand still long enough for your sister to squeeze you." Her voice was positively fluttering with joy, with anticipation, with love for Andrew, for Christmas, for life. "Where's Richard?"

"Why? You want to kiss him, too?"

"Maybe." She could not stop smiling. "I just sort of wondered where he was."

Richard was a year and a half younger than Andrew, who was eight, and from the time he'd been able to walk Richard had trailed Andrew as if he were following a rainbow. Andrew seemed to find this just and agreeable. He preferred his brother to any of his friends, and the two of them inhabited a world to which others, if they behaved, were welcome, and from which, if they did not, they were quietly evicted. This world, in addition to the two boys, was occupied solely by animals. Hector, the German shepherd, ostensibly the family's, was theirs. The guppies, the turtles, and sometimes it seemed the birds in the trees, all theirs. They had dozens of puppets —alligator, monkey, owl, fox, cat, rooster—who performed frequently and did not require an audience, though there often was one. Andrew and Richard extended this love of nature to plants. They had a cactus garden in their room, and were always nursing some doomed avocado pit. The yard outside was broadcast with seeds that rarely brought forth fruit—everything from olive pit to mango was rescued from the garbage and given its chance to live again, without reference to climate. Last year they'd produced three exquisite little gourds and a recognizable pumpkin that was made into a jack-o'-lantern and only relinquished when Mr. Perry gave them a choice between "me and that decaying grin over there, one of us must go!"

In Andrew's and Richard's world, the law for lamb and lion was friendship, and they and the sun rose eagerly each day scarcely able to wait being about the business of living. Mr. and Mrs. Perry and Barbara, partly baffled, partly awed, entirely captivated, thought there'd probably never been any other such two since the beginning of time.

"I'd be stunned and grateful even to have known *one,*" Mr. Perry had said more than once. "But *two*. And living right here in the house with us—" He'd shake his head and look at his wife and daughter as if expecting some explanation, knowing that they no more than he could give one.

Now Andrew looked up at his sister and said, "Richard's in the cellar, making scenery."

"Andrew, can't you remember to call it the rumpus room? We spent two hundred and fifty dollars making it not a cellar."

"Yeah, that's right. He's in the rumpus room making scenery."

"Puppet show tomorrow?"

"At two o'clock." He added with the shy smile of a creator, "It's gonna be pretty good, Barby. You'll like it."

"I like them all. They're marvelous."

"Yes," he admitted. "But this is even better. You'll see. I made a new puppet in school."

"Oh? What's it of?"

"A jackal," Andrew said happily. "You'll love him,

Barb. Well, I have to go now. Richard's waiting for me to help." He gave her a wave and sprang down the stairs, like one of his own animals into a burrow.

Barbara went to the kitchen, where her mother was rolling pie crust. "Those kids," she said, sitting down at the table with a little snort of amusement. "Now they're going to make us love a jackal."

"I believe it. All I can say is thank heaven for puppets. We'd have to move to a zoo or something. Did you notice it's snowing?"

"Sure," said Barbara, attempting to sound offhand. Now that the snow was assured (it was coming down heavily, thick and dry) and her evening was assured, she preferred to deny, even in her own mind, its importance. Between now and eight o'clock there was much to be done, but eight o'clock would come and it was—what? Secreter? *Safer?* More fun?—She wasn't quite sure, but something in her now wanted to ignore the evening, as one ignores a gift held in someone's hand but not yet proffered. You know it is for you, you pretend not to see, until "Here, this is for you," is said, and you take it and reply, "REALLY? For *me*?" in a pattern formal as a ballet. Her evening to be was that sort of gift.

"Anything I can do here?" she asked, offering distraction more than help.

"Well . . . I'm making pie for tonight and one for tomorrow, but that's practically done. Tonight's dinner is too easy to start now. You could clear up the stuff here, if you like." Mrs. Perry waved at pots, pans, floury rolling pin. "Listen, let's have a pot of tea first. You make it, and I'll be through here by then, and we can just sit for a bit." Her forehead wrinkled. "Heaven knows what I've been doing all day, with only two pies to show for it."

"Don't forget the centerpiece."

"Oh, the centerpiece. I guess we better had. Forget it. I almost went out for a poinsettia, only I do hate to admit I have a poinsettia mind. Except, of course, that I *do* like poinsettias, and there really isn't anything wrong with that."

Barbara smiled. "Didn't the magazine mention poinsettias?"

"Heavens, no. Gilded nuts and dead rhododendrons and lots of spiky things and nothing going together but everything marching. . . . I don't know how they do it."

"A poinsettia wouldn't make a very good centerpiece. We wouldn't be able to see each other."

"We could have put it on the sideboard," her mother pointed out. "Except that then it wouldn't be a centerpiece, of course. Let's have some of that spice cake from yesterday, if there's any left. Oh, now here comes your father. We'll have to share."

"That's the way I like to be greeted," Mr. Perry said. His shirt collar was open, his tie pulled to one side, he had a pencil behind his ear. "On Christmas Eve, especially. Gives you that feeling that after all Christmas has deeper meaning than the exchange of things bought for money." He sat down, reached for a piece of spice cake. "Has either of you noticed that it's getting to be sort of fashionable not to like Christmas?"

"Lots of people don't," Letty Perry said slowly. "When you consider some aspects of it, it's no wonder."

"What I mean is, nobody used to *say* it. Practically nobody. Now a day doesn't pass from the beginning of December that somebody doesn't tell me he hates Christmas. And did you see that card we got this morning? All wreaths on the front and candles, and then inside it said *Merry Christmas and All That Garbage*. I don't like things like that."

"Well, that's just bad taste," Mrs. Perry said, stirring her tea. "We only got one like that."

"Still," he insisted, "it seems to be getting fashionable. And I object. I don't mean to do anything about it, mind. Just want to go on record as objecting."

"Sometimes I wonder why I ever wonder where Andrew and Richard came from," Mrs. Perry said, and she leaned across the table to give her husband's hand a quick squeeze before settling back to her tea.

Barbara, looking at the two of them, wondered why *she* ever wondered about Andrew and Richard. I'm the misfit in this family, she thought. For it was perfectly true that in their way, her father and mother were as remarkable as her two young brothers. She lived in a house with four people who seemed to know and be at peace with themselves, who seemed to live rich full lives in an inexpensive brown frame house set on a rather unkempt quarter acre on the edge of a small Ohio town. (And they weren't absolute fools about it, so you couldn't even complain on that score.) Any sort of questionnaire answered by Mr. and Mrs. Perry could only be dull. Ordinary address, ordinary number of children, ordinary health, wants and credit references. To *Occupation* her mother would always answer Housewife, her father, Teacher. Never would her mother be able to write Actress, Architect, Ballerina, or her father casually scribble Physician, Journalist, Cabinet Member. Didn't they ever miss and mourn the lost chances, the missed careers? Didn't they ever long to be something more than Housewife, Teacher?

It would appear that they did not, and Barbara, who loved them, understood them no more than she did the two boys now painting scenery in the rumpus room. She wanted to be an actress, an architect, a ballerina, physician, journalist, cabinet member and a few other things besides, and none of them in this town, yet it crossed her mind from time to time that she could become all these things and the few others besides and still not turn out to be as happy as Andrew and Richard, who were undoubtedly going to be veterinarians in Ohio.

"The trouble," her father was going on, "with Christmas is that people, with the exception of children—and not all of them—don't have illusions about it any more. They don't seem to have illusions about much of anything any more. I think people without illusions are poor right into their bones. A world of poor people, that's what we're breeding."

"You seem to have quite a few," Barbara said curiously, enviously. "More than I have."

"And will not relinquish them. But I'm in the minority. You," he added, "are at the proper age for losing illusions. With perseverance, you can probably get most of yours back in a few years. People of my grandfather's generation got them back almost automatically. My father probably put up a struggle, but he managed. With me it's been a pitched battle, and Lord knows what your generation will do. You understand I'm generalizing. Have we finished all the spice cake?"

Barbara and Mrs. Perry smiled. "I don't know what you mean, we," his wife said. "There were only two pieces, and you've eaten them both."

Mr. Perry lifted one eyebrow. "Did I? Sorry about that." He reached up a hand to rub his neck—a gesture of apology with him—knocked the pencil from behind his ear, leaned over to pick it up, straightened and resumed, "The point is it's all gotten too commercial. That's what people say. And I'll grant you it's pretty commercial, and cards like that are an outrage, but so what? Throw out the card, and let the commercialism go on in the stores, that doesn't mean it has to worm its way into the home, does it?" He looked at them, and shook his head. "Of course not. We don't have great commercial Christmases here, do we? Enough to make me nervous about the bills in January, but that's as it should be. But we have—" he spread his hands "—very *nice* Christmases."

"Puppet shows," Barbara said.

"Exactly," said her father with approval. "That's what I mean. Well—" He pushed his chair back. "I suppose I should get back to work." In his spare time Mr. Perry was writing a history text for sixth-graders. It was frankly a matter of supplementing their income and despite his illusions Mr. Perry tended to grow cynical about any value beyond that in the book. "What happens," he had once explained, "is that I find myself wondering, Why say that to sixth-graders, and then of course I say, Why say that to anybody? and that leads to enormous questions like, What's the use? And then where am I? Except behind in my income tax, of course."

"Why don't you write a book that will make a lot of money?" Barbara asked now.

"My dear child, how do you think I maintain these illusions we've been talking about?"

"Well, how do you?"

"By not asking too much. Of life, or of myself. I could not write a book that will make a lot of money, so I spare myself—and the rest of us—grief and disappointment by not attempting to."

"What would you do if you did make a lot?"

"Pay off Sears, Roebuck," said her father and got to his feet. Barbara looked after his retreating back, turned to find her mother laughing. "I don't think it's so funny," she muttered.

"Oh, neither do I, I suppose," said Mrs. Perry. "But *he* is." She began to gather dishes, put them back on the table. "You're doing this part, aren't you? I guess I could start dinner now. We'll have an early one, and that'll give you time to get dressed without rushing."

Barbara, who still wished to see her evening obliquely, said, "What are we having for dinner?"

"Everything that's left in the icebox. I'll heat it, of course."

"That's nice. That you're going to heat it, I mean."

Mrs. Perry, who was a confirmed list and sign maker, studied her daughter a moment, took a piece of paper and printed carefully: THIS IS SMOVATNA. IT'S AN OLD ARABIC RECIPE AND I DON'T WANT ANY COMMENTS ON IT. She took this message into the dining room and put it on the table, came back to the kitchen and said, "There. Now, tomorrow we'll start all fresh."

The sound of Mr. Perry's typewriter was heard distantly from a little space upstairs which had once been a sewing room, which he used as a study, since Mrs. Perry didn't sew enough to appropriate a room to that use. (She'd been known to say, "Richard, your pocket is torn. Hand me a safety pin and I'll sew it up.") Subdued sounds of triumph came from downstairs as the scenery painting progressed, and a periodic drumming as Hector's heavy tail hit the wallboard in its wagging. Mrs. Perry hummed, tossing leftovers into the top of a double boiler. I have such a nice family, Barbara thought. It's no wonder I get depressed occasionally. She listened to the snow purr against the window over the sink, and allowed her eyes to rest directly on her evening. "This is for you," said an aerial voice. The voice of what? Oh, of youth, of longing, of wonder. "This is for you, Barbara." "Really?" she murmured, but not aloud. "It's really for me?"

But she'd known it was for her.

CHAPTER TWO

*The rest of the house was what you might call comfort-*able—certainly not furnished in any particular style. A powerful old sofa that even Hector couldn't wreck, several easy chairs, big tables usually strewn with books and magazines. "Early Frenetic," Mr. Perry was apt to call it, or, "Twentieth Century Periodical." The living-room rug had been bought before Barbara was born, and looked it. There was no rug at all in the dining room, but they had managed, a few years earlier, to have the halls and the stairway carpeted. Last year they'd turned the basement into a combination rumpus-television room, and Barbara had vague plans of giving a party there. But her own room was different, not like the rest of the house at all. A bright, butter-colored room that almost satisfied Barbara's love of symmetry. Two of everything. Beds, chairs, tables, two of each. Two pictures precisely hung and so alike as to be almost identical—they were street scenes of Paris. Only one bureau, but with everything on top in pairs and so arranged that a jar at one side was balanced by its mate at the other. ("With a room like this, you should have the most even disposition in the world," her father had said once. Barbara smiled at him and thought, It's all very well for people to say he's marvelous. They don't have to put up with that sort of thing.) She came into the room now, having finished her bath, and smiled at it as fondly as one of her brothers might have smiled at a kitten. A very neat, yellow kitten, she said to herself. It was the sort of thing the room put her in mind of, even on a cold winter night—yellow kittens, marigolds, strawstacks sunning, honey. . . .

She got out her black ski pants, her ponyskin snow boots, a thick white sweater. She brushed her hair hard, then smoothed it into a page boy, put a trace of pale pink lipstick on her mouth. Yes, one day she might give a party in the rumpus room, as her mother and father suggested, but—this was such a very big but—she knew something they didn't know. She knew something she thought perhaps nobody else knew, except possibly some girls at school, who wouldn't be interested. And this was that she was not very popular. *There,* she thought, as this piece of intelligence took form in her mind and settled slowly to the bottom of her stomach in a hard lump. *There's* honesty for you. To be truthful, she wasn't entirely sure of her unpopularity. It was a conviction she had, which was belied by her appearance and general behavior. Certainly she looked and acted like a popular girl and so was taken for one, and anyone who troubled to wonder would probably assume she was popular with somebody else. Was that what she meant? She meant that she couldn't really think of enough people she knew well enough, who, she felt, liked her well enough, to make up even a moderate-sized party for a moderate-sized rumpus room. And if you couldn't do that, could you call yourself liked? Even if you did have sufficient acquaintances with whom to go to ball games, with whom to dance at the high-school Fortnightlies (to which people did not go in couples), if you made and received enough phone calls so that there was no reason for embarrassment on that score, still you knew in your own heart that that was not popularity, that was not being really well liked. When Margaret Obemeyer came into a room, people brightened, there was an automatic movement toward her, and it seemed that everybody had been just waiting for her to show up because there was something they had to tell her, ask her. Because they just liked having her around. Andrew—more than Richard—had this quality of heightening the spirits, the sensibilities even, of people around him. Andrew was absolutely adored by his teachers, and was also adored by his classmates, who telephoned him constantly, invited him to parties, on picnics, to their homes. Sometimes he went, more often he did not, preferring to be with Richard.

But the choice was his. Nobody seemed to like him less for refusals, and he didn't like anyone less for making them. Her mother and father . . . they weren't especially party people, but they had a lot of friends. People liked them, liked them very much indeed. You could tell it the second you saw them in company. But what did Margaret and Andrew and her father and mother do? What did they have or know that made them so comfortable in the world? So apparently unafraid of what people were going to think? Why should they be afraid? she asked herself a little sourly, but added, How did they get so they didn't need to be?

I don't know, she thought, turning away from the trim, symmetrical bureau, I'd give anything to know, but I don't. I'm always nervous about what people are going to think of me, say of me. All this so-called analyzing right now is just because I'm getting nervy about tonight and being with that gang and maybe not singing right or maybe saying the wrong things or giving myself away somehow. Giving herself away *how?* Well, that too, she didn't know. It was a way of putting something she couldn't word. It was why she didn't really know whether she was unliked or merely withdrawn. Maybe people would like her a lot if she weren't so afraid of finding out. "*Barbara Perry? Why, she's a lovely girl, just lovely. It's a pity she's so shy. You can tell she—*" Tell she what?

Oh, stop, stop, *stop* . . . Barbara said to herself. Her pulse was fluttery and she definitely was beginning a headache. But it's all nerves. It's a *crise,* she informed herself loftily. Barbara belonged to the French Club. She also belonged to the Drama Society (props), to the Pep Club (when there was an out-of-town game she went along with a crowd in the bus and helped yell from the bleachers), to the tenth-grade basketball team (not the varsity). She was not shunned, not a pariah. Always, if she wanted it, there was someone to walk with, to sit with at lunchtime, in the study hall, someone to telephone if she felt like talking or wanted to go to a movie. Now and then a boy would take her to the Friday night movie in town to which all the young people went and virtually no adults. But an arrangement like that never lasted. It wasn't that she quarreled with these boys, nor they with her. They just sort of stopped asking, and Barbara didn't care, and if they chanced to meet in school, in town, on later occasions, there was a perfectly cordial exchange of greetings.

Oh, but it's all so *bloodless,* she thought now, in entreaty, in rebellion. Is this the way things are going to be forever? *Forever?*

She looked at the clock.

It was time, it was past time, for them to have arrived. A familiar, a detestable feeling of apprehension began a slow seizure of her limbs, and she felt it coming, like a patient resigned to a recurrent disease. Despair she might, but resigned she must be, since it happened every single time she had an appointment, either to meet or be met by anyone not in her family. If her father said he was going to meet her downtown, he met her. If her mother said she'd stop by the school and pick her up, she stopped by. There was never any doubt there. But these arrangements to see people of her own age. . . . Oh, agony. Wouldn't it be better, really, to give up all attempts to be popular, give over all making of dates, and so be spared this terrible process of misgiving at a minute's lateness, anxiety for five minutes after that and utter panic if the delay continued up to ten? No use to tell herself she never had been actually forgotten, that any delays had been unavoidable, quite forgivable, quite infrequent. Each time was new. It didn't matter what had happened before . . . this time they'd started out and just overlooked the part about picking up Barbara Perry.

Grudgingly her eyes moved to the clock, darted away appalled, and the ice settled in her spine.

She got up and walked around the room. It doesn't matter. It doesn't matter at all. What difference does one evening make in a person's life? What difference, for that matter, does one person's life make in the world? You could be miserable, rejected, jilted, overlooked, your whole life long, and it really wouldn't make any difference, except to you, and you were just one person, and one person didn't make any difference—

"Barbara? *Oh,* Barbara!"

"Yes, Dad?" she called from her door, her voice mild, incurious. He could be calling for any number of—

"The Irwins are here."

Safe! "All right, Dad. I'll be right down." Freed from dread, she shed it unthinkingly, flew to the mirror, patted her hair, leaned forward to study a moment the rose-flushed face, left the room with one soft bed lamp glowing to greet her on her return.

Jeff Irwin was a six-foot fifteen-year-old with a voice, Barbara thought, like the oldest frog in the pond. He even resembled a frog, in a sort of handsome way. As if he'd been on his way to becoming the prince and had gotten interrupted.

"Another three months," he was telling Barbara's parents, "I'll be old enough to get a license myself. Then Dad won't have to play taxi all the time—"

Chug-a-rum, said Barbara to herself.

Mr. Perry said, "I'd have been glad to drive tonight, if—"

"Oh, crimers, Mr. Perry. I didn't mean that." Jeff frowned enormously. "Hi, Barbara, meet my father. Does it go the other way around? I can't ever remember who gets introduced to who. Anyway, this is my father and that's Barbara Perry." Mr. Irwin started to speak, but Jeff was hurrying on, "For Pete's sake, Mr. Perry, I didn't mean—"

"Relax, Jeff," his father said. "We fathers know we're just a bunch of cab drivers." He grinned at Mr. Perry. "That right?"

"Well, it seems the fathers of the boys get more than

their share," Mr. Perry said. "Got your snow tires on?"

"Yup. We'll need them. This is coming down pretty heavy."

"I could pick up some of them after the caroling, if that'd help."

"It's all arranged," Jeff said. "Randy Lawson's father is picking us up at Connie's."

Mrs. Perry asked what time that would be, and Jeff said he wasn't sure. "But don't you worry, Mrs. Perry. We'll get her home all right. Around eleven. Something like that."

Mr. and Mrs. Perry smiled. You could tell they liked Jeff.

So there it is again, thought Barbara, going out into the snowy night with the Irwins. I look at Jeff and think of a frog-prince. My parents look at him and think—what? That he's a nice reliable boy, obviously. That they like him. Right away, just like that. Mr. Irwin didn't look at me that way. I'm just another of the kids he has to pick up on his route tonight, that's all. By tomorrow he wouldn't be able to recognize me, probably.

She sighed a little and then took a deep breath and for a moment forgot herself. It was so beautiful. A white world, an air filled with torn frozen lace that drifted against them as they walked to the car. Up and down the street the houses were decorated with Christmas lights, and on some of the lawns lighted trees bent their branches gently, heavily. A car with a broken skid chain clanked by, feeling its way, and when it had passed the only sound was that of snow falling into snow.

"Golly," Barbara breathed.

"Yeah," said Jeff. "Pretty, isn't it?"

"I just hope it lets up pretty soon," Mr. Irwin said, opening the back door of the car and gesturing them in. "You people are going to get snowbound somewhere if it doesn't." He'd left the motor of his car running, and the interior was warm and snug.

"That wouldn't be so bad," Jeff said in his low croak. "Wouldn't mind getting snowbound at Connie Frost's. Say," he interrupted himself, "that's a good one. Snowbound at the Frosts'." Mr. Irwin chuckled with what seemed actual amusement, and, a little belatedly, Barbara tossed her chuckle in. "But with all those records she has," Jeff was going on, "to say nothing of the way they stock that refrigerator, why snow-binding would be a pleasure. I suppose you'd call it snow-binding?"

Mr. Irwin was too busy trying to see the road to make any comment, so that left it up to Barbara. For the life of her she could think of nothing to reply except, "Sounds reasonable, I suppose."

Jeff looked at her a bit gloomily, sat forward on the seat to direct his father. "You take the next left, and then down in the middle, just about, that's Maxwells'. You wait here, Dad. I can run right in and grab old Max. He said he'd be ready and waiting." He occupied the remaining time to the Maxwells' house with unnecessary directions to his father, and Barbara sat in a corner, feeling her *crise* worsen. Only why should I feel that I'm the one found wanting in this interchange? she asked herself angrily. He was just saying the silliest sort of things. Why should I be made to feel stiff and ungracious because of that?

Mr. Irwin said, "Haven't seen you in quite a while, Barbara. How've you been?"

Barbara started, and hoped he hadn't seen her. "Just fine, Mr. Irwin," she said. Had she gushed? Oh well. . . . "Just dandy. And you?"

"Tiptop. You know, this is a pretty night. And that's one of the ways you know you're old. Soon's you start hating the snow, you're on the downward path."

If this had been her father, she'd have said, "Chin up, Dad. You're keeping wondrous well." But she could scarcely say that to Mr. Irwin, and she couldn't think of anything else to say. Taking a deep breath, she began, "Well, golly, Mr. Irwin—" And then, thank heaven, Max and Jeff were there.

They crowded into the back seat, and Jeff said, "You two know each other?" just as his father said, "Where to now, boy?" Max and Barbara admitted they'd met, and Jeff gave his father more directions, and they drove on.

They picked up Margaret Obemeyer, who was wearing a hooded scarlet parka and ski pants. "My tomorrow's Christmas present," she admitted when Jeff and Max whistled. "Hi, Barb. Aren't you glad it snowed?"

"Am I ever," Barbara said, and immediately lapsed into silence. Why do I *say* things like that? she wondered despairingly. What is the matter with me?

Jeff was saying, "You look like what started all that trouble in Chicago one time."

"A cow, wasn't it?" said Margaret. "How're you, Mr. Irwin? It's awfully nice of you to drive us. And on such a night, too."

Why didn't I think to say that? Barbara asked herself.

"I was thinking of the flame," said Jeff.

"Don't mind in the least," said Mr. Irwin. "It's such a pretty night."

They stopped for Randy Lawson and then drove to the Frosts', from whose house the fun and caroling were to begin.

There were eight of them to go caroling (Bud Parker and Alice Ordway had already arrived), but there seemed to be many more people in the Frosts' living room. A positive crush of people. Barbara's vision was a little blurred, whether from cold or nervousness she scarcely troubled to wonder. Her eyes often did this to her—glazed a scene so that she couldn't quite take it in. But all these people . . . and then she quieted and some of them turned out to be adults. The Frosts must be having a party of their own or something. Barbara turned to Margaret Obemeyer, as the only person she really knew. The only person, she amended, she really knew to be friendly.

"When are we going to start?" she asked.

"What? Oh, practically right away, I suppose. Randy, you do have the carol booklets, don't you? Who has the can for the money?"

"I do," said Connie. "Oh, hi, Barbara. Nice you could come." She moved over to Jeff, stood almost under his chin (as if, Barbara thought, she were trying to get under an umbrella) and murmured, "That was a wonderful touchdown you made the other day, Jeffy."

"*Touchdown?* That was basketball we were playing," he said on a croak of laughter.

Connie smiled. "Only made it more thrilling. You want to carry this?" She thrust a decorated container at him. "For the money. You're so good at arithmetic and all."

"What's she giving me this snow job for?" Jeff demanded of Randy.

"Search me," Randy said. "She either likes you or she's afraid that thing's going to blow up."

Jeff shook the can. "Sounds harmless. I'll look into the other matter."

"Children," said Mrs. Frost, coming into the group near the door, "do remember you're all coming back here for chocolate and cake afterward."

"Would you like a do remember from me, Mother?" Connie asked.

"Oh, goodness. I forgot. *Young people,* do remember you're coming back here for chocolate and cake afterward. Is that better?"

Connie looked around at her friends. "She still manages to make it sound like children, doesn't she?"

"If you baked the cake, Mrs. Frost," said Max, "you are hereby given permission to call us wee mites, if you want to."

"By all means I want to," said Mrs. Frost. "I'll begin with Jeff here," and she tipped her head backward and smiled up at Jeff. She and her daughter were both small, and they took, it seemed to Barbara, every opportunity to point it up. As if the rest of us were giants, or something.

"Listen, let's get going, shall we?" Margaret asked. "We're supposed to sing at twenty houses, or maybe it's thirty."

"Twenty or thirty?" someone yelped. "We'll have our windpipes frostbitten."

"Well, we don't have to—"

"Come on, will you, if we're gonna get started—"

"Where's my scarf? Somebody took my— Oh, here it is—"

"Why do I have to know arithmetic, anyway? Just have to hand the money to Mrs. Howard, don't I?"

"Children! Hurry up, you're freezing us, leaving the door open that way!"

They were outside, pale breath hovering in the snowy

air, snow crunching beneath their boots, nestling on their hair. Snow . . . snow . . . the snowiest world imaginable. Piled thick and white on roofs, on telegraph poles and mailboxes and porch railings, swirling up steps unchecked, unshoveled. Street lamps hung like balloons of gauze, and wires ran overhead fuzzed with white. Laughing, already cold, sparkling with pleasure, they trudged down the street to a large brick house, like a house on a greeting card with its enormous wreath of holly on white double doors, its windows alight, its ivied walls frosted so that only a leaf here and there thrust out like a dark little flag. Through French windows they could see a great tree looped, furbished, emblazoned with tinsel, with balls, with lights bright as jellies. Assembling near the windows, they held their books in mittened hands and began . . .

O Come, O Come, Emanuel . . . they sang, and the people of the house came to watch them, to listen, smiling and friendly. A man reached over and opened the windows. *Away in a manger, no crib for his head, the little Lord Jesus lay down his sweet head.* . . . They sang four carols and then amidst greetings received a donation, the windows were closed, and they moved on up the street to the next house.

Angels o'er the fields. . . . O Holy Night. . . . Deck the hall with boughs of holly. . . .

They went from house to house and sang and received money and moved on, getting colder, their voices getting weaker. But it was lovely. Barbara thought she couldn't remember ever before doing a thing so . . . friendly and spirited, so gracious. She shared a book with Randy Lawson, liking the look of his big homemade mittens next to her smaller fur ones, the sound of his deep boy's baritone mingling with her soprano. She'd known Randy—known everyone in this group—for years. A knowing free from intimacy, that involved no more than nods, an occasional word spoken in passing. Six of these people were members of a larger clique, one very powerful in school. There was no use, her father said, in deploring cliques. Barbara forebore to point out that she didn't deplore them, she only wanted to be in one.

"The human being is by nature cliquish, clannish," he said. "It wants to feel different, elected, but not by itself. In a group of other human beings different and elected in precisely the same way. It wants arcana, and the secret grip, and the special references that make it not part of the human race, but part of a very distinct part of the human race. Then it feels safe. Nobody *really* wants to be an individual. Not if it means giving up his place in the clan."

Her father tended to talk that way, but did he know that his own daughter was as yet uncliqued, unclanned? That she shared the arcana and special references of youth only in the largest way, not in the minute specific way that she and everyone her age (perhaps everyone of every age) longed for?

I don't want to be an individual, she thought as she sang *The First Noel,* I want to be part of a gang, part of a gang like this. I want people like Margaret to save a place for me at lunch, and people like Randy to ask me to the movies on Friday night. I want to be with them not because Mrs. Howard suggested it and they're good-natured about suggestions, but because they want me, Barbara, to share with them. Well, she was with them now—the great, the envied ones. All except Bud Parker, of course, now holding a book with Alice. He apparently had also been chosen by Mrs. Howard. She had probably done it alphabetically, and so the accident of the alphabet had placed her and Bud with this group tonight. She spared a moment to be grateful that she hadn't somehow wound up sharing a carol book with him.

O Come, O Come, Emanuel. . . .

They were back to the beginning of their repertoire.

"Listen," said Margaret as they finished and moved away from the nineteenth house, "I hate to give up, and I won't if everybody else doesn't want to, but I'm freezing."

"Me too," said several voices at once.

"Tell you what let's do," Jeff boomed, stamping his feet and slapping his arms around his broad chest, "let's do one more to make it even and then go back to Connie's and jump into a nice hot cocoa."

"Good idea—"

"I *can't*."

"Oh, one more won't hurt. Think of the Heart Association."

"Right now I'm thinking about my own heart. It's an icicle."

"When isn't it?"

"Oh come on, let's go. One more burst of song and—"

"*Excelsior!*"

They moved on.

Twenty minutes later they were tramping up the kitchen steps at the Frosts', kicking off boots and galoshes in the cold rear porch.

"Take your jackets and things inside," Connie directed. "Shake them off first. Because if you leave them out here they'll be like suits of armor." She led the way into the kitchen.

It was big, with curly-maple cabinets, copper pans and molds hanging on racks, philodendron in brass pots hanging from the ceiling, a Dutch oven in the wall. The sort of kitchen my mother will always dream about, Barbara thought. And dreaming's as close as she'll ever get, with Dad so careful of his illusions. It seemed funny—a man with her father's brains to be nothing more than a history instructor. Wouldn't you think—

"Wow!" said Max. "Look at that cake, will you!"

They looked at the cake. Gorgeous, huge, frosted with chocolate, bedizened with blanched almonds, absolutely whole.

"Can we eat the entire thing?" Jeff asked, advancing on it with outspread hands.

"*We* can," Connie said pointedly. "By *we* I mean all of us here forgathered, not *one* of us."

"Oh, I'm gonna share," Jeff protested. "You know me, Connie. Everybody's friend."

"This is a lovely kitchen," Barbara said.

"Glad you—" Connie began. "Jeff! Get *away* from that cake! Help get out saucers and things. Cups and spoons."

Margaret was already at one of the cupboards, and Alice at a drawer, as people who knew a room well. Barbara helped arrange cups and saucers around the big table and listened to the laughter and conversation that hovered and swooped and dove around the room like birds. She didn't speak, but tried to make her silence appear lighthearted and interested, the silence of one who could contribute much but on the other hand doesn't have to be chattering every moment to prove it. "*Barbara Perry? Oh, Barbara's one of those rare people who doesn't have to be talking every moment just to hear herself talking, but don't let that silence of hers fool you. Why, she—*"

"Barbara? Don't you want a piece of cake? Well, pass your plate, girl." Was there a trace of impatience in Connie's voice?

"Sorry," said Barbara.

And that was wrong, too. But how did you manage if

you didn't yet know (might never get to know?) the secret grip, the stupid arcana (why did she keep remembering that word?), the special references? If you tried to listen—brightly, attentively silent—to catch the flow and so perhaps be caught up in it, somebody snapped at you . . . well, not to say snapped, but still—

"Boy, you *are* a dreamy one," said Randy, at her side. "Here's some cocoa. What's on your mind?"

"Nothing, really. I mean, I'm sort of thawing out, I guess."

He sat down, put his chin on his fists and stared at her. "Mind if I watch?"

"Watch what?" she asked with an anxious laugh.

"The thawing process. I like to see girls thaw."

"Look out for that guy," Jeff warned. "His remarks seem so harmless—and then that's what they turn out to be. It's terrible."

"Blow," said Randy, from the side of his mouth.

Now why did she find that so inexpressibly appealing? The combination, perhaps, of his blond, his almost downy good looks, and the tough word. But why didn't she say something? She smiled unhappily, liking him, wanting so much to communicate with him in some way, utterly unable to.

"I was thinking about my uncle," she blurted.

"Your uncle?" Randy looked astonished. He turned to the others and said, "Here's a girl thinking about her uncle." All eyes were immediately on Barbara.

"Uncle?"

"Why, for heaven's sake?"

"What *about* your uncle?"

"Well, I've heard of lots of original things to do, but—"

"Come on, come on," Randy pleaded. "What were you thinking about your uncle?"

"Well," said Barbara, a little breathlessly—she was about to steal one of her father's pieces of whimsey and only hoped she could do as well with it as he did—"Well, he's living with us. Only right now he's a German shepherd—" If nobody picked her up, she was lost.

But Randy—he really was marvelous—frowned and said, "Poor fellow. How did he get in this condition?"

"He lost an argument with a witch over transformation."

There was a burst of laughter, and Barbara, smiling happily, went on, "Now he's very busy trying to get back, only he doesn't know how."

"It'll have to be witchcraft, that's clear," said Randy.

"Runes, or something," Margaret said.

"He could recite something backward," Jeff mused. "Beard's *History*. Something hard."

"Could he stick pins in a toy cat?" Connie asked.

"Don't be repugnant," Alice protested. "Anyway, how would he hold the pins?"

"The thing is," Max said, "is he really *trying* to get back, or do you just think he is?"

"Bending over backward," Barbara said.

"Maybe he should be bending frontward, then."

"That's right," said Randy. "These spells, you never know how they'll take you."

Giddy with success, Barbara relinquished her Uncle Hector to their care, and they were on their second cup of cocoa before they abandoned him, with shaking heads and bursts of giggles, and went on to a discussion of the Drama Society's spring offering, *Pomander Walk.*

Barbara, feeling warm and snug, listened in attentive silence. Once she glanced at Bud Parker, finding on his face the expression of frozen felicity that she knew too well, and she thought she should talk to him. As one of the safe, the accepted ones, she should talk to him, draw him into the flow. But she hardened her heart and looked away. She wasn't that safe and accepted, not by a long shot, and she was not about to align herself with another outsider and so risk . . . risk what? She couldn't say what it was she'd be risking, but whatever it was, she wouldn't. She didn't look at him again until they were leaving, and then only to say good-by.

CHAPTER THREE

She lay awake a long time that night, hands behind her head, a little smile on her lips, thinking over the evening, thinking of Randy's face, recalling the inflection of a voice, the turn of a phrase, remembering—against her will—Bud's dark, still features. Forget him, she told herself. My goodness, you aren't responsible for . . . She summoned up Randy's face again. They'd driven home in his father's car, and as chance had it Barbara was the last to be dropped. She and Randy were in the back seat alone for a few blocks. They talked to each other and Mr. Lawson contributed nothing. In fact, Mr. Lawson didn't say more than hello and good-by the entire trip. He was quite unlike Mr. Irwin. Not taciturn, exactly. Barbara decided maybe he was preoccupied, and forgot him. She asked Randy, "What does Mr. Irwin do? I seem to remember him from somewhere—"

"He works in Hogan's Pharmacy."

"Oh, sure." Now she remembered. Mr. Irwin was a pharmacist, and Hogan's was one of those drugstores where you couldn't get anything but medicine, so Barbara scarcely ever went there. But sometimes with her mother, and once in a while alone, Barbara had been in to have prescriptions filled. And he'd remembered her, while without his white coat she could never have placed him. "Does he remember everybody's name?" she asked.

"Oh, he's a real friendly guy, Mr. Irwin," said Randy. His glance strayed to his father, returned hastily to Barbara, and he said, "That was fun tonight, wasn't it?"

"Oh, lovely," she sighed. "I did so like it."

"Great." He pulled his gloves off and slapped them together, placed them carefully on his knees. "Now, don't misunderstand me," he said, his voice a little loud. "I don't mean everybody's gotta be friendly. I just happened to mention Mr. Irwin's that type. Sort of friendly."

"He seems to be," Barbara said, a bit bewildered. Then she understood. Randy was talking to his father, not to her. It was one of those subterranean family things, and, as clearly as though she'd heard it, Barbara could devise the conversation that took place in their home from time to time, with Mrs. Lawson saying, "I don't see why you can't be a little more friendly with Randy's friends," and Mr. Lawson saying, "I drive them, don't I?

What more do you want?" and Randy saying, "Nothing, Dad. It's fine . . . I mean, I'm satisfied. It's nice of you to drive us." You couldn't tell, from this brief, one-sided familial exchange in the car, whether Mr. Lawson was a really unfriendly man, who made his wife and son—she didn't know whether Randy had brothers or sisters—unhappy, or whether he was just a quiet type who didn't have anything to say to Randy's friends. All she was sure of was that Randy wasn't paying attention to her, Barbara Perry, when he spoke. He was figuring what to say to his father when she left, and he was a bit tense about it.

Now she lay in bed, and the smile left her lips. That'd be awful, to have to worry so about what to say to your parents. Probably his mother was all right . . . practically nobody had two parents who were difficult. And I have two who aren't, she thought. I'm really very lucky, except I never stop to think about it. Practically never. She wasn't as she had been for so long, blindly uncritical of them. In the last two or three years, along with the peculiar personal problems that had seemed to assail her all at once, she had realized that her father and mother had faults. But if you compared them with other parents, they came out well. Her greatest grievance against them was that they never seemed to be serious enough about anything, they were too *good*-natured. Put in words, it sounded like a ridiculous complaint, but Barbara knew what she meant. It was aggravating to live in a house where the two younger members always found life meaningful, the two older ones always found it interesting, and there you were all by yourself in the middle finding it at times so arid and at times so grim as to be only just bearable. Andrew and Richard you could forgive—even if you couldn't understand them—because they were so young. And her father and mother weren't fools—they didn't really think life was brimming with good fair fun and jolly incidents. Her mother, for instance, was shocked and grieved when Hungary was occupied, but she did not, as Barbara tended to do (when she thought of it at all), brood uselessly over orphaned children and hungry and suffering people. She organized a drive to send money and clothes and she worked hard and didn't talk about it. Her father frequently got depressed about the unhappy condition of the teaching profession. Less forceful than her mother, all he did was talk about it. He'd come home and say, "You know, driving along of a beautiful fall evening, a man gets reflecting. There's nature all around him . . . the sky is that chewing-gum gray and all the roadside bushes are bursting with discarded Kleenex . . . well, a man gets to pondering over human nature, and then over the things that go on in the name of Education, and I tell you, his heart beats in his throat and the tears start to his eyes. . . ." Then he'd sigh and rub his neck and ask his wife to repeat everything she'd thought since two that afternoon, leaving out fantasy. "Reality," he'd say, "that's what I'm after. Did you ever hear what the patient said to the analyst? 'If it weren't for reality, Doctor, I'd be perfectly all right.' It's this sort of thing I'm trying to forget, so just give the facts, please."

Didn't either of them ever want to swear, or slam a door, or say something that would have to be apologized for later on? Apparently not, thought their daughter, and held it against them. Not all the time, not even often, but once in a while and sharply.

CHAPTER FOUR

"A sandwich," Mr. Perry exclaimed. "Just what I wanted."

Andrew laughed. "It isn't a sandwich. It's a notebook."

Mr. Perry examined his gift carefully. Two wooden covers, a pad of paper between, a pencil attached by green string, and all done by hand. "So it is," he said. "It'll be just the thing for my desk, I believe."

"I thought it'd be just the thing," Andrew said comfortably. He never had any doubts about presents, either the ones he gave or the ones he received. The fact that a thing was a present put it in a category that admitted of no criticism or misgiving. Richard, on the other hand, inclined to be diffident, here as elsewhere. You would not, his mother thought, call him meek, or submissive. It was just that Richard was unassuming about life, reserved about people, words, presents. About everything, really, except animals, with whom he had apparently come to terms. Where Andrew zestfully, and of course often wrongly, assumed that everything was for the best, Richard preferred to wait and see. She remembered a time when Richard had come home and announced that he was in the first-grade play.

"Pandora," he'd said in his soft voice. "A play about Pandora."

"Oh, I know that one," Mrs. Perry had said. "What comes out of the box?"

"Hope," he said seriously. "And a lot of troubles."

"What are you, darling?" she'd asked with a little laugh compounded of love and tenderness. You always loved your children—but they had moments of appeal that transcended day-by-day emotions, moments to which you responded with a rapt, unpremeditated joy that was like a sudden flooding of sunlight.

"I'm a trouble," he'd said.

"A bad one?"

He debated, then shook his head. "No, just an ordinary trouble."

Oh, darling, she'd said, but only in her mind, you are so like yourself. And I love you so.

Yes, she thought on this Christmas morning, looking at the brilliant litter of paper and boxes, at the tree, whose little lights seemed pallid in the sun- and snow-struck brightness of the morning, at her two sons and her daughter and husband, still in robes and slippers—because who'd think of getting dressed on Christmas morning—yes, Andrew and Richard are themselves in every bit of their beings. She didn't know what good fairy had stood at each of these cradles and said, "He shall be at home with himself," but it was what had happened to them. A mother could only be awed and grateful—and only in a little part for herself. It was for what it meant to them, these two boys who would one day be men, that she felt humble and thankful.

Hal and I aren't like that, she thought, glancing at her husband, who was drinking cold coffee and trying Barbara's tie on over his pajamas. I guess we're stable and adjusted, somewhat. We know what love is. We are fortunate people, and we know it. But Hal's a compromiser with life. He's even something of a cynic, if a good-natured one. And I? I'm a woman who likes asparagus fern but throws it out, and not even for so understandable a reason as that everybody does. I do because I'm not sure that the stuff isn't, after all, perfectly horrible and I'm just not able to see it. "Discard the asparagus," the magazine article had directed. "It's too too silly, and besides it sheds." So I obediently discard it, and feel resentful and wonder where my convictions are. In so many ways I am unsure of my own judgment. I go about thinking, *Do I dare,* and *Is it right?* and more often than I can let Hal or the children see, I simply do not know.

The books on child psychology—and she had read countless such books, all firmly contradicting each other—agreed on this, that you must know your own mind, your own course, before attempting to lead your children. "Do not say no unless you are clear as to the *reasons* for the no. This only leads to a possibility of having to reverse yourself later on, thus losing face with yourself and confusing the child." Easy enough to say bosh, to tell yourself that psychiatrists' children were invariably the worst of the lot. There was truth in what they said. You *should* know your reasons, know your mind, if you were to guide another human being through the labyrinth of childhood to successful maturity—to even a reasonable facsimile thereof.

I hate that word *should,* she thought now. It's like something standing over you with a whip. Never lashing out, just standing there, the whip loose in its grip, flicking slightly. The almighty *should.* And I'm forever saying no without thinking, thus having to reverse myself and so lose face and so confuse my children. I must have lost a thousand faces by now, and confused them beyond any possibility of repair. And yet . . . there were Andrew and Richard, glad of life. What more could anyone ask in the world than joy in living, with whatever it offers? I must have had some part in making them so.

The phone rang and Barbara moved to answer it. She

almost sauntered, the very picture of a girl uninterested in the telephone, but her face was tense, and when she heard the voice at the other end she stiffened slightly.

"This is me . . . she . . ." she said, and waited. "Yes, sure, Bud. . . . No, not at all, it's very nice of you. . . . Lovely, just lovely. Christmas is such a . . . Yes, that's what I was going to say, it's such a lovely day. . . ." There was a longer pause, during which Barbara twisted the phone wire, looked irritably at the ceiling. Mrs. Perry knew, in part, what her daughter was thinking, and she decided to phone the telephone company in the morning. An extension in the rumpus room, in the sewing room, in a closet if necessary, but the extension must be obtained. Heaven knew, it would be a convenience for all of them, not just for—

Barbara said, "I'm sorry, I can't. No, it isn't that—I . . . I have to sit with my brothers on Friday. . . . Mom and Dad are going out—" She avoided looking at her family as she said this. "Yes . . . well, I'm sorry too, but you know how it is. . . . Yes, g'by, Bud."

She hung up, sauntered back to the chair around which her gifts were piled, then said defensively, "What could I say? I'm sorry but I don't want to go to the movies with you? Isn't it nicer to say I have to sit, or something? Anyway, you may want to go out Friday. How do you know you won't?"

"Who said anything?" Mr. Perry asked. "It seems a

reasonable enough excuse. Kind enough. What's the matter with the fellow?"

"Nothing. I just don't want to go out with him."

"Well, that's for you to decide." He looked at his sons, who were examining Andrew's magic set. "Not that I approve of lying, even kindly lying, but there are times—" He broke off, shrugged. They weren't listening, anyway.

"Mother," Barbara said, *"can't* we get an extension? It's positively uncivilized, having to stand there talking with everyone and his brother listening in—"

"I was just thinking about it," Mrs. Perry said. "Tomorrow, darling. I'll phone for sure."

Barbara looked disgruntled still, and Mrs. Perry thought she could scarcely be blamed. I must have said a dozen times I'd have an extension put in, and somehow kept putting it off, for one reason or another. For no reason, really. I just forgot. But it's important to Barbara, and wouldn't you think I could have made that simple effort? Barbara, in these past couple of years, has been so difficult to please, so often unreasonable. But wanting another place to talk on the phone is not unreasonable.

"I'm sorry, darling," she said. "I mean to, but I keep putting it off. You'd think I really had a lot to do, the way I lose track of things."

"Oh well . . ." Barbara said. She meant it to be gracious. "This is a beautiful sweater, Mom. Maybe I'll go up and try it on." She stood, gathered her presents, smiled at her parents and said, "It was a beautiful Christmas, really."

"What do you mean, was?" Andrew asked, not looking up from the intricacies of a dismembered puzzle box that he was attempting to reassemble. "It's not over. We got hours yet, and the puppet show."

"I guess I mean the presents part," Barbara said. Her voice trembled a little. "Leave it to me to find Christmas in the getting." She went out of the room, her chin up, slender back rigid.

Mr. and Mrs. Perry looked at each other, a silent exchange of glances that said much, but, Mrs. Perry thought, answered nothing. "Want some more coffee?" she sighed.

"Sure, Letty. Okay." He got up, patted Richard's head and went into the kitchen, where the breakfast dishes were untouched. Shoving a few aside to clear a place for the two of them, he put a light under the coffeepot, and turned as his wife entered. "I was talking to Ted Palmer the other day," he said. "Remember him? Fellow in the medical school."

"Dr. Palmer. Yes, I remember him."

She poured two cups of coffee and they sat down, drew up their chairs. It crossed her mind that they were behaving like people about to have a conference, and it made her a little nervous. Why did the prospect of serious conversation, even when it was needed, even when it was welcome, always vaguely alarm her? She supposed it was something left over from childhood, when the teacher asked you to remain after class a few minutes. Or perhaps it reminded her of the moment after the examination when you sat down with the doctor to find out what he'd found out, or what part of it he proposed to tell you. It wasn't that she wouldn't face things, or try to face them, it was just that this initial flutter of resistance preceded serious moments, and it had been that way her whole life long. She wondered if Barbara felt that way, if possibly it would explain why she rarely would discuss things that troubled her. At least, Mrs. Perry amended, won't discuss it with us. Does she, perhaps, with her friends? Her teachers?

"Maybe it's just that she doesn't want to talk with us," she said suddenly. "Some children don't, you know. In fact, I remember I never would with my mother, not about anything serious, anything really close to me. That is, I wouldn't after I got into my adoles—into my teens. Before that it was all right. And after that. It was all right with Barbara, really, until the last couple of years. Three years. What about Ted Palmer?"

"He says his daughter is the same way. I was just asking him, sort of generally, you know, about adolescents— What's the matter?"

"Nothing. It's just a . . . silly reaction to a word. I don't like the word."

"Why not?"

"I don't know. Too clinical, maybe."

Hal frowned, made an incomplete gesture with his hands. "Well . . . call it youths, then. I was asking him about youths." His wife smiled. "He said that his daughter was the way I was saying Barbara was. Thin-skinned, all wrapped up in herself, moody. Palmer says what lots of us overlook, or don't know, is that it's a matter of simple hormones in many cases. Not that hormones are simple, of course. But that it's not so much a personality conflict as a hormone imbalance. Temporary imbalance. And some of these—youths—take an awful beating during this period and all anyone can do is wait it out. Do what you can to help, but don't go into a tailspin because Johnny forgets all the manners he ever learned and Sally bursts into tears if you say it's sunny out."

"You're quoting Dr. Palmer?"

Mr. Perry nodded. "Thought it might help."

"Well, it does. In a way. But it's just that I . . . I feel so *sorry* for her."

"So do I," said her husband, shaking his head. "And that makes three of us, because she sure feels sorry for herself."

CHAPTER FIVE

By that time Barbara had stopped feeling sorry for herself. She had come upstairs hurt and angry, whether with them or herself she didn't stop to wonder, but she wondered, very seriously, why she was always getting into this predicament of feeling both wrong and wronged. Anyone could make her feel this way. A teacher, a stranger (with merely a *glance*), Bud Parker, her brothers, her parents. Whether or not they meant to—and she supposed, if she had to be honest, they usually did not—people so easily made her feel misused and mistaken.

Bud Parker, now . . . why had he had to call her? Because he thought it would be easy to persuade her to go to the movies, and maybe one of the other girls would be harder? Or had he called one or more of the others and been refused? I refused him, too, she reminded herself. Yes, but in her refusal there was that—oh, how in the world to put it?—that slightly frantic note of apology. As if she had no right to refuse anyone who asked her anything. And saying she had to sit with her brothers. Why not just a dignified refusal? "No, Bud, I'm sorry, but I have other plans." "No, thank you so much for calling, but I won't be able to." Why explain? And explain wrong, at that.

But it was always the same. Not just with dates that she didn't want. People asked unreasonable things of her, and she never knew what to do except comply. That Mrs. Mumford, the English teacher, who'd say, "Barbara, *would* you mind on your lunch hour just popping over to the drugstore and picking up a bottle of aspirin for me? I just never seem to have *time*—" Seething, resentful, all smiles, she'd go, wasting half her lunch hour, and why? Because I have absolutely no character, she told herself now. Mrs. Mumford could get her own darn aspirin and not louse up my lunch hour to save herself a few minutes and a short trip, but I haven't enough spunk to say, "Sorry, but I promised to meet Katy Stryker at lunch and go over some work with her." And so then I come rushing in late to meet Katy, and she's annoyed, and when I explain that I had to get aspirin for Mrs. Mumford, she reminds me that last time it was because I was taking some papers down to the office for Sonia Bemis, class secretary, who couldn't quite make it then herself and gosh, Barbara, if you *would,* it'd be an enormous help, thanks, kid, and what had Sonia been doing? Keeping a date with a quarterback probably. If you were even slightly dumber and could convince yourself you were the generous type who adored being imposed upon, it would be easier. This way you just felt furious and helpless, and you heard yourself, over and over, saying, "Not at all. I'm *glad* to help." You—you *hypocrite,* you.

Barbara, lying on her bed among her presents, narrowed her eyes at this unpleasant picture. Have I always been like this? I don't seem to remember a time when I wasn't uncertain, but it wasn't always this bad. I can remember when I was young and didn't want to go to parties (I can't remember why I didn't . . . but I never did like parties much) I'd just say so. I'd lie, and say my mother wanted me to do something else, or I was going somewhere with my father, but I would say no if I didn't want to go. When did I begin to have to say yes to all requests, or suffer this way if I managed to say no? And don't fool yourself, she added grimly, you're feeling this way because you refused a date and now maybe Bud won't like you. What difference does it make if he does or doesn't? That's beside the point. Whether or not it makes a difference it makes you nervous to think anyone might not like you. And then Andrew makes some remark that sets you off, and here you are, on Christmas Day, glooming in your tent.

But after a while this mood of remorseful introspection passed, and she began to examine the sweater her mother had given her. Orlon, soft as cashmere, lavender, with a fake turtle neck. It should be divine with her purple plaid skirt and a narrow lilac ribbon in her hair, which she wore long and let those who would crop theirs till they looked like violinists à la Capp. Some girls had no sense of femininity. Even Margaret Obemeyer was sort of that way, with her short hair, short nails, her tendency to wear jeans whenever she possibly could. But Margaret was an awfully nice girl. She'd said something last night about getting together, but of course you couldn't tell what that meant. Something or nothing . . . anybody's guess. Why did it have to be Bud who called? They'd all had fun together last night, laughing and singing and talking. Randy had gotten a kick out of Uncle Hector, and Max had. Why couldn't one of them have called and said, "How about the movies Friday night, Barbara?" Unwillingly, she remembered again Bud's quiet features. Well, my gosh, if I went out with him, I wouldn't stand a chance of being accepted by that crowd. He isn't one of them, and I'd be marked as an outsider. To be perfectly fair, so would he, with me. So in a way I'm doing him a favor. *Oh, come off it,* Barbara, she said to herself, in one of her moments of irritable honesty. If you have to be a hypocrite, at least you can be an honest one.

That made her smile a little. It was a nicely turned phrase. At times, Barbara felt she'd rather like to be a writer one day. "Barbara Perry? Oh, I read every word she writes. Isn't she fabulous? So much *feeling,* and understanding . . . I just don't see how she does it." Barbara Perry, speaking at the Women's Club in town, making a flying visit between New York and California. "But she *always* stops here, in her home town, and I think it's perfectly wonderful, considering the demands on her time." An exquisitely cut black cashmere suit, Italian silk scarf at her throat, elegant pointed Italian pumps. "But of *course* I remember you . . . Randy—Randy *Lawson. How* good to see you. . . . Oh, do you remember the night we all went caroling in the snow? . . . But I would *love* to sign it for you—" Her own book, her sixth, a world-wide best seller. "To Randy with affectionate—no, cordial—recollections . . . Barbara Perry."

Once she had gone to the Women's Club with her mother when a woman writer was giving a talk. Very famous and dowdy she'd been, quite a disappointment. Still, after the talk Barbara had gone up to her and confessed her own ambition to be a writer and asked for advice. The woman had really been extremely absent-minded, preoccupied. Her eyes barely rested on Barbara, and she said, "All the advice I ever give—or ever received—is write a lot and read a lot and then write a lot." Probably she'd meant it to be pithy. Barbara, stung to retort, had said, "Oh, I don't mind the writing part, but reading does really make me melancholy . . . I mean, I can't even read a long *letter*—" The woman had blinked, smiled remotely, turned away. Barbara flushed now, remembering. But women that age often didn't like girls . . . too much reminders of their lost youth or something.

She decided to wear the purple plaid skirt, the lavender sweater, the narrow lilac ribbon, for attendance at the puppet show. It would have been nice, she thought as she dressed, if Randy or Jeff had called. Or if Margaret or Alice had. "Barbara? This is Margaret. I was wonder-if you would—" What? Oh, anything at all. If she'd go skating with them, or to a taffy pull, a hayride. "I was wondering if you'd like to go burgle a house with us tonight?" "Oh, I'd love to, Margaret. What time shall we start?" Anything, anything. . . . She giggled a little and then stopped, rebuking herself. Get to giggling out loud by yourself and the first thing you know you're crazy, unreal.

But that, she told herself, standing before the mirror and brushing her hair, is the crux of the whole thing. She put the brush down and leaned forward, looking at that girl. *She* may be real, but I'm not. She had this sensation from time to time, when she felt eerily vague, so filled with lassitude that it was like being disembodied. With a little shiver she turned away. Using almost defiantly deliberate motions, she began to tidy the room. If you did something practical, something objective that required movement and produced results, the other feeling passed away, usually without your noticing when it went.

So . . . the two slips, the new gloves, the handkerchief from Richard (with a picture of Peter Rabbit hiding in the watering can) went into her dresser, the home-made candle from Andrew on top. The camel's-hair coat, darling of her heart, was carefully hung in the closet and the box that had contained it went under her bed. You never could tell when a nice big box like that would come in handy. Gathering up the other boxes and tissue paper, she stood looking around a moment. Was that all? Was there something else, something she was forgetting? A moment of standing, or searching with her eyes, brought no answer, so she went downstairs.

In the living room her father was burning paper and boxes in the fireplace. The Christmas dross made a beautiful blaze, and Barbara, handing her share over, said, "Isn't it strange . . . it's all so lovely, so briefly, and then it's nothing but ashes." She stopped, suddenly hearing the words. It had been as if someone else had spoken for her, but as if she'd known it would happen. How peculiar. "Did you know I was going to say that?" she asked her father.

He glanced over at her, drew the firescreen, and said, "I knew—expected—you'd say something of the sort."

"Why?"

"Because, honey . . . you think in dramatic ways."

"Trite, you mean."

"Drama's very often trite. After all, the human race has been around a long time. Everything's trite, really. Doesn't make life and drama less important that they're . . . known."

"Known?"

"Repetitious. Often predictable."

"I suppose not," Barbara said, sitting down. "Where's everybody else?"

Her father took another chair, began to fill his pipe. "Your mother's upstairs dressing. The boys are downstairs, seeing to the last-minute details, I guess." He struck a match on the bottom of his shoe, puffed a lazy cloud of smoke into the air and seemed to come to a decision. "Barbara . . . is something troubling you? Something, that is, that you could talk over? Maybe I could help." He avoided looking at her, as if a direct glance would send her flying, but she could feel his concern, something that came from the center of his being and reached toward the center of hers.

There was a time, Barbara thought, when I went to him with everything. The broken doll, the shattered myth, the crumbled hope . . . all the pieces carried to this man, who mended things, or, if he couldn't mend, could help make a loss endurable. That wasn't so awfully long ago, she cried in desperate silence. And he's the same man—gentle, understanding—who gave me a Santa Claus who was joy and love and who didn't need to drive a sleigh across the sky to exist. He gave me that Santa Claus and gave me belief in him. He consoled me when I wept over the extinction of dinosaurs (the beautiful, dumb, plant-eating dinosaurs she'd loved so when she was six and had somehow located in Greenland, where she planned to visit them one day) when my first-grade teacher, with a sentence, swept them from the world and left it desolate. He stayed up with me for hours, or all night, that year when horrible dreams, hooded and hot and squatty, sat in my room waiting for me to go to bed, knowing that then they'd have me, but underestimating the power I had in reserve—this man. My father.

He's the same man.

So why can't I tell him how I feel formless and unloved and lost, and that I don't know how it happened? I can't, she realized wearily, because I'm not the same girl. Adolescence—she used the word indifferently, it served its purpose—is a disease. And you can't blame anybody, not your parents, not even yourself. Nobody elects to be diseased, but nobody, either, comes along and injects you with a hypodermic full of it. Surer than mumps or measles it gets you. Only when you had mumps and measles you were little and could cry and carry on and accept the ice cream and the toys and the devoted attention, and all that was your due. This thing—this illness that seized everybody, only some got sicker than others—came too late, lasted too long, was too personal and indescribable for remedies. All you could do was suffer and wait and hope you wouldn't be scarred for life. And you couldn't say any of this to your father.

You couldn't, either, turn away his offer without comment, which was your first impulse. So—"There's nothing wrong, really. I mean, everybody's got something wrong, but it all straightens out in time, doesn't it?"

He lifted quizzical brows and shook his head slowly, not so much in denial as in defeat. "Well, I don't know how to answer that. Except, no—it all doesn't straighten out in time. I suppose most things do. Sometimes it helps to talk."

"I don't have anything to talk about. No problem, I mean."

They looked at each other in bafflement. But it *was* baffling. She looked at him, knocking the tobacco out of his pipe now, and placing it carefully in an old blackened rack, relic of a Christmas long past. He was the same man and her feelings for him hadn't changed, but something had, and she supposed neither he nor her mother believed she really still loved them. How could they, when she behaved around the house practically like a stranger who's been unwillingly detained, who puts up with the family customs, attempts to observe them with as good grace as he can muster, but who is essentially not of this place? Did she feel that way, or only act that way? It was difficult sometimes to sort out which was which, what you really felt, what you pretended to feel, and what was feeling thrust upon you that you could neither relinquish nor accept.

The living-room windows were decorated with snowflakes and frost flowers made by the boys. Barbara stared at them, thinking how pretty they were, remembering the afternoon a couple of weeks ago when Andrew and Richard, with sponges, stencils and some sort of cleaning powder, had set to work with the earnest concentration they brought to any job.

"Is this a snowflake, Andy? Or a star?" Richard held a stencil out to his brother.

"Snowflake," said Andrew, examining and returning it. "Put it in that corner. Put sort of half of it, like it was coming around the corner." Andrew was no particular lover of symmetry.

"Do they really look like this?" Richard asked as he worked.

"Sure."

"Let's go out and get some and see."

"They're too little," Andrew said after a pause. "You couldn't see."

"Little? There's snow all over everywhere."

"Then it's too big. Or too stuck together. You couldn't see. But that's how they look."

In silence Richard applied half a snowflake to the corner of the pane. Then, "Who makes the snow, Andrew?"

"God," said his brother promptly.

"Does he make everything?"

Andrew nodded.

"Mountains?" Richard persisted. "And people, and mice, and kangaroos and—"

"Everything," Andrew said, as the list grew.

"I know one thing he doesn't make," Richard said slyly.

"What's that?"

"Beds."

The two of them doubled in laughter, and now Barbara's lips quivered a little, remembering.

"What are you smiling at?" her father asked.

"Oh . . . the boys. They're . . . I don't know. Amazing, incredible. How did they get like this, do you suppose?"

Mr. Perry said slowly, "I imagine a good deal of it is due to your mother. She . . . she's basically a person who's glad to be alive. I suppose she communicates that to the boys. It's a magnificent gift."

"Then why doesn't she communicate it to me?" Barbara burst out before she thought. She'd have taken it back, if there'd been any way. As it was, she bit her lip and hoped her father would overlook it, knowing he would not.

They sat in silence for a moment. The clock in the dining room struck the half-hour. Across the street an automobile horn blew in front of the Murrays' house. Ellen Murray, Barbara thought, being called for by her fiancé, who didn't have enough manners to get out of the car and go up to the door. Ellen was seventeen, engaged, and was going to get married as soon as she graduated from high school in June. I wouldn't be her for all the rice in China, Barbara thought. "How much rice do you suppose there is in China?" she asked her father.

He shrugged. "That's like wondering where the hill of beans is that nobody knows anything from. What wouldn't you want for all the rice in China?"

"To be Ellen Murray, getting married at seventeen."

"It's young," her father said, clearly not interested in Ellen at the moment, though he was usually willing to be drawn into a discussion of human motives, no matter whose. "This is how I see it—" he began, and Barbara knew he did not refer to Ellen. She had a sudden conviction that in this manner her father would begin one of his classes. He was not a man to *tell* people. He'd say *This is how I see it,* and show you how he did, and then delicately, determinedly elicit a view from you, his daughter, his students, whomever he happened to be talking to. Well, I'm not a classroom, she thought, setting up a defense before he'd even begun. I can't get up and walk away, but he isn't going to draw me out. She did not ask herself why she took this position, but prepared to defend it, if she could.

"This is how I see it—and I've thought about it a lot, Barbara. Your mother, even though she lets herself get imposed on a lot—oh, yes, she does—these women in town inveigle her into taking over jobs they don't want, and she does them, partly because she doesn't know how to refuse, but mostly because impositions on her can only be superficial because essentially she has this--I don't know exactly what to call it, except a joy of living, a *willingness* to take everything involved in living, including tiresome jobs that other people feel too grand for or too busy for— She's always had this quality, only when you were small, and I was away in the Navy, it was sort of submerged. She was lonely for me, I guess, and very young to be alone with a child. Almost too conscientious. I remember she used to write me letters telling me what this book said and that book said about the rearing of children. She didn't have a family and she didn't have a husband with her, and I suppose she was just too serious, poring over her books, trying to do the right things without stopping to trust her instincts. Is this making sense?"

Barbara, uncomfortable, reluctantly interested, shook her head, then nodded.

"I'd write and tell her to throw the books away and be herself, and she'd write back and say she didn't know precisely who herself was and at least the people who wrote the books didn't seem to suffer from uncertainty—"

She said that? Barbara thought. And then, Well, it's interesting that she's given the boys her joy of living and me her sense of uncertainty. She listened to her father in silence, hoping he'd stop pretty soon.

"Do you see what I'm getting at?" he asked.

"In a way," she said. He waited, so she went on unwillingly, "I guess I do, Dad. Only I wish you wouldn't try to make me *say* things about it. Can't I just think about it instead?"

"Of course, Barbara. You asked me something about the boys, and I thought—" He broke off, and Barbara thought there were things she should say. He was a kind, wonderful man who was trying to help her, and here she sat, sort of numb and stiff, recognizing a lot but unable to put anything in words. Unwilling? Well, it came to the same thing, really. She did not like intimate discussions with her family, and, though she would have welcomed a chance to have intimate discussions with a friend, there was no such friend to have them with.

Katy Stryker? Oh no, not Katy, who was stimulating, but—harsh, somehow. Moreover, you couldn't have a two-way conversation with Katy, who never thought of anyone but herself. She pictured herself and Margaret Obemeyer, spending the night together at one of their houses, doing their nails perhaps, and talking things over. They'd be such good friends that they could discuss anything . . . not just boys and sex, though those would certainly form a part of their evening's communication, but things like this business with her father. She could hear herself saying, "And so there was my mother, young and all, and *uncertain*—you know how you get—" Margaret would nod "—so she really was, you know, serious to a positively handicapping degree, and then when my father got back, I was practically four and he had to look for a job and finish his M.A., and they really were awfully poor—" Would she say that? Yes, to this friend (Margaret, probably) she would say anything "—poor, and what with this and that she still didn't have time to show this natural love of life she has—and she does have it—but the uncertainty . . . I mean, you could have knocked me down with a feather when my father said that about her writing and saying she wasn't sure who herself was, because I get that feeling so much. . . . And then, well, I suppose by the time the boys were born things were more settled and all. . . ." Yes, she could hear herself, going on and on, confident of understanding. . . .

She didn't know she had sighed until she heard her father echo it. And still there was nothing she could do or say.

She got up. "I suppose I could get at the dishes."

"That's an idea," he agreed pleasantly. "Meant to say, the sweater looks very pretty. It's a nice outfit."

"Thank you, Dad." She stood uncertainly a moment, and he helped her out by looking around for the paper. "Even if it is Christmas," he said, and glanced at the floor, as though he could see through it to the rumpus room. The boys objected to normal pursuits on holidays. "Are you going to read the paper *today*?" Andrew had said to him on Thanksgiving, almost as if he had proposed going in to teach a class to an empty room. Special days implied special behavior, in Andrew's mind, and he was prepared to impose this view on others.

"If you hear them coming upstairs," Mr. Perry said, settling and getting out his glasses, "hoot like an owl."

Barbara, relieved and disappointed, went into the kitchen. She hadn't wanted him to pursue the conversation, but still—

She stacked the dishes, ran hot sudsy water in the dishpan, slid the silver into it and dreamily sloshed a sponge over forks, knives, spoons. She didn't mind doing the dishes. She didn't mind housework at all. Katy Stryker was forever in trouble with her parents because she wouldn't help around the house at all. But not at all. "She won't do a single blessed thing," Barbara had heard Mrs. Stryker say, at a bridge luncheon here one day. The ladies were still at the luncheon part (though, in truth, when they got the game going they talked pretty much as steadily) and were discussing their children. There was a general air of dissatisfaction, and Barbara, who'd been crossing the hall upstairs, had sat down on the floor and eavesdropped without compunction.

"All the times I've said to her, 'Katy, you live in this house, you might at least make some contribution,' and she goes right on looking at television or pretending she has homework to do when she's just lying there on the bed staring at the ceiling and when I say something she says she has a stomach-ache, and what can parents *do*?"

"I don't know, I'm sure," Mrs. Fillmore had said. "I yell at Hortense and yell at Howy, and all I get is blank stares. A great big boy like Howy, and who shovels the snow? I do."

"Oh, you *don't*—"

"I do. Who's going to?"

"I'd let it pile up to the second-story window."

"And have the milkman or someone break his leg and sue me? I don't understand children these days. Howy never directly *refuses* me, you know. He just simply doesn't *do* anything. I don't know . . . what can I do? He's practically six feet tall. I can't take a hairbrush to him." Mrs. Fillmore was a widow and her voice was always stretched over a whine. It must be tough on her, Barbara had thought. Howy Fillmore would do any darn old thing he was asked to, around school. Worked like a fiend for the Drama Society, would show up in the gym to decorate for Fortnightlies and be right in there pitching. So what got into him at home, that he wouldn't lift a finger to help his widowed mother? Well, who could tell?

She set the silver on the drainboard, ran hot water over it, got a dishtowel and began to dry. I don't know what gets into people like Howy and Katy that they simply cannot bring themselves to help. I've told Katy that it's easier to do the dishes, or run the vacuum, or whatever, than get involved in constant arguments. Katy says housework interferes with her thinking. With her dreaming, she means. She wants to lie there and dream and make up things and maybe think, too. But how can you concentrate on daydreams if your mother's grinding in and out of the room yelling at you every second? It's better to do the things. Then they leave you alone. And Howy? Well, maybe he's selfish and maybe he's lazy, but there is more to it than that. She wondered what would have happened if she'd given in to her impulse that day and called down the stairs, "Why don't you try not yelling at them for a change, Mrs. Fillmore?" Pandemonium and outrage, and her mother furious with her. And her mother would have been right, too. It wouldn't only have been rude, it would have been pointless, because from all she could gather Mrs. Fillmore had been yelling for years, and she sure wouldn't be about to stop because somebody Howy's own age gave her a piece of insolent advice, even if the advice had merit as well as insolence.

Well, my mother doesn't yell, and I don't refuse to do housework, and why that doesn't make everything smooth and pleasant between us is more than I can answer. Maybe wanting everything smooth was asking too much, but why didn't it lessen, to some extent, the sense of remoteness, of indifference, that Barbara felt about the house? Because the truth was, she didn't take much pride in the house, except her own room, of course. How could she? It was shabby and worn. Clean, but when had it last been painted, inside or out? All right, they had done the rumpus room, but wouldn't you think they could manage new slipcovers, a decent rug for the living room, a decent lawn outside instead of that stretch of crabgrass and dandelions? The house was okay . . . but nothing you could take pride in, and she did her share of the housework in order to avoid fuss, period.

You could dream very handily, doing dishes, or you could sort of blank out your mind, slumped on one hip, conscious that your eyes were stary and unfocused, your hands lolling in the dish water, only occasionally coming to grips with a plate or a fork. A sort of Midwest version of navel contemplation that could go on until the water got tepid, the suds flat and someone came in the kitchen to jar you back to earth with a sentence, or even a footstep. While it lasted it was the closest thing to disconnection with the world that you could have and still be awake.

She remembered that as a child—like many children before her and since—she would at times begin spinning and keep on until she staggered through a loosely tilting world in which she had no place of security, no knowledge of direction. She'd never been able to figure out just why she—or any child—would do this . . . throw the clockwork of the world completely out of gear, so that ceiling and floor went whirling and chairs swam away or loomed up from nowhere and you bumped your shins and fell against things and finally had to close your eyes and hang your head until the spinning darkness slowed and slowed and at length stopped and you were safe to look at a world grown steady again. This trance above the dishpan was rather like that. Not so deliberate or violent, but the same in the sort of crazily loosened sensation you got, as if you'd been sitting at the center of a wheel and had suddenly let go and been thrown into space.

And that day Mrs. Fillmore had said to the listening women around the luncheon table, "I said to him, 'Howy, for mercy's sake, if you don't want to think of yourself and your own character, could you at least think of your sister? What sort of example are you to Hortense?' And do you know what he said? He said, 'Whyn't you let me be an object lesson to her, Ma? Wouldn't that do?' "

There was an appropriately indignant gasp from the ladies, but Barbara, stifling a giggle on the second floor, had distinctly heard her mother laugh before she composed herself and said, "Oh my, that must have been trying."

Mother's all right, Barbara thought, and Dad is. With a mixture of condescension and penetration, she found words for them in her mind. Bright and creative and earnest and honest. All of those. What was wrong between them and her, the incommunicability, the frequent, inexplicable tensions, was all her fault. Yes, she thought, satisfied—indeed, quite moved—by this feeling of humility. It isn't their fault that I am detached, that I am different, that life in a little Ohio town can never be enough for me.

"Heaven knows," she said to an imaginary interlocutor, "I didn't ask to be this way, driven by ambition's spur toward distant, shimmering goals." *What ambition? What goal?* I do not know the goal, she cried. Only its distance, its brightness. She refused to answer the first part of the question. After all, at fifteen you needn't have everything solved. She did well at school. She was going to college. There was lots of time to decide *what* she wanted to be, to do. *Where* was more important, and the one thing she was sure of was that it would be a long way east or a long way west of here. Oh, she would come back . . . always, because this was her home and her family was here, she would come back, a bird of passage, loving and loyal in spite of her success. Furred and fragrant, she swept into the house (completely remodeled and redecorated, at her expense, but the same old house) "Barbara Perry was born in there, in that very house, and do you know, she still comes back, every chance she gets . . ."—and opened her arms to them. "Mom, Dad . . . oh, it's so *good* to see you—" And her brothers . . . those two divine-looking tall men, who were such wonderful veterinarians (she would have preferred to have them doctors, but even in someone else's dreams Andrew and Richard could not be made into anything but veterinarians) and so much adored by their sister. "Oh, but my *brothers*," she said to the interviewer from the *Times*, "my brothers are men of the earth, they are like great strong trees, their roots deep in the soil of home." Of course, for the purposes of that interview, it would have been better if they'd all been brought up in Nebraska.

Ohio didn't sound rooty enough. On the other hand, that would mean that at this very moment they'd be *living* in Nebraska, and that was going a little far, even as a place to get away from in order to refer to lovingly when you'd reached the pinnacle of success and didn't need to live there any more.

Dishtowel in hand, she reached toward the drainboard, found nothing to dry and realized with vague surprise that the dishes were finished. I keep telling Katy: You can dream yourself into a stupor doing housework, and nobody bothers you. (Katy always said, "Once and for all, Barbara, I'm not dreaming, I'm *thinking*." It was never said once and for all, and Barbara never really believed her.) She's awfully stubborn, and she has a strong character. You'd have to have a strong character to keep lying on your bed trying to dream, or think, when your mother was saying every fifteen minutes that if you lived in the house you ought to make a contribution.

"Don't you think maybe you should?" Barbara had asked her once, in the hesitant voice she used for anything resembling criticism of her friends.

"Why?" Katy had asked, adding, "I do do some things. But a lot of that junk is stuff she could perfectly well do. She's around the house all day."

Barbara, who would neither wish to nor consider talking about her own mother that way, was still rather awed by Katy's indifference to her parents. Katy often claimed that she wasn't their child at all. "I'm adopted," she'd say calmly. "I'm no more their child than—than you are." The first time she heard this, Barbara said, without stopping to think, "But that's silly." She was slightly unnerved by the glance Katy gave her, but it remained one of the few times she refused to take a statement back by qualifying and propitiating—her usual method when she found herself in disagreement with anyone outside her family. But it just was such a silly thing to say.

"I suppose you think nobody ever got adopted and not told?" Katy had asked.

"Well, sure, but . . . But you'd *know.* Wouldn't you?"

"That's just what I'm telling you. I do know. They haven't the courage to tell me. Poor things," she added imperiously.

"*How* do you know?" Barbara asked, in utter fascination.

"My blood tells me. My instinct. My true heritage tells me. I can remember the first time I knew it. It was a couple of years ago, and I was driven mad by do this, do that, do this, do that, and all of it squalid like emptying the garbage or cleaning that wretched parakeet's cage, and my father sitting there in his chair getting fatter by the minute—"

"By the minute?" Barbara faltered.

"He *won't* go on a diet. He's a fat man and he won't even try and I can't stand the sight of him. Don't you think people should take some pride in themselves?"

Barbara released her caught breath and nodded. But to say you couldn't stand the sight of your own father . . .

"Do you want to hear this, or don't you?" Katy asked, though nothing could have stopped her from going on. "Well, then, listen. There he is, the jolly fat man, saying why don't you help your mother out, she works hard enough for you—not that he ever lifts a finger except to get a second helping—and Mother yakking and yakking and *yakking* about how did a child of theirs ever get so ungrateful, and suddenly I *knew*. I got up and walked out of the house and downtown and all the time I was walking I was thinking, *So that's it . . . of course.* I'd been blind, and now it was crystal clear. I wasn't their child at all. Oh, it was a stupendous feeling."

"I should think you'd have been miserable."

"Miserable? Miserable! I was free. It was the truth and it set me free." She swept the air with an impatient hand. "What do I care how they carry on about ingratitude and why don't I contribute? They're nothing to me, and I'm nothing to them."

Barbara didn't know how much of this Katy believed. She'd never expanded on it quite so much again. Just occasionally, when the going got extremely rough in the Stryker household and Katy found herself forced either to contribute or go without her allowance and without dates, did she mutter, "What do I care? I'm adopted. They just won't admit it."

Barbara wondered whether Katy had ever confronted them with this theory. She didn't ask, but would have bet anything Katy hadn't. She also wondered, and did not ask, how Katy could justify to herself staying in the house, accepting the help and support (which she got, whether or not she was willing to admit it) of two people she disclaimed and despised.

As a matter of fact, with Katy you couldn't be sure whether in her mind she really did disclaim and despise them, or whether this was another part of her general fierceness toward life. "Do you think your kid sister is adopted too?" she'd asked Katy once, and received a contemptuous glance. "Fay is quite obviously her parents' child. You only have to look at her." To be sure, Fay looked a good deal more like the Strykers than Katy did. Katy was an enigma, and Barbara vacillated between discomfort and pleasure at having had the friendship of this girl conferred upon her. Conferred was the word for it. Barbara never would have selected Katy for a friend, but Katy had done the selecting and Barbara had been quite helpless, as she was with all strong-minded people, to resist. She supposed she didn't even want to. Katy had an air about her almost certain to be attractive to a self-doubter like Barbara—an unquestioning assurance that went well with her bold carven features, her graceful, almost haughty carriage.

Katy was not especially popular in school either, but you knew that with Katy it was a matter of choice. She chose to ignore most people, so naturally they didn't take to her. But if Katy had wanted it, Barbara believed she could have had the whole school, with a crook of her finger and a smile, at her side. That, of course, Barbara recognized as a supposition, based on Katy's tremendous good looks. The fact that she accorded deep reverence to beauty did not blind Barbara to the truth that beauty was not enough. It was one of the ambivalences in her thinking that disturbed her, and about which she could do nothing. She'd think, Anyone as beautiful as Katy can do what she wants with life, and the thought would not be finished before she'd add, What can beauty do when it's mixed with so much ugly thinking? She didn't really see an awful lot of Katy. Not nearly so much, for instance, as Margaret Obemeyer and Alice Ordway saw of each other. But they ate lunch together a few times a week, and Katy came to the Perrys' to visit fairly frequently. Barbara rarely went to the Strykers', because Katy rarely asked her.

"Let's go to your house," she'd say, if there was a decision to spend the afternoon, or the evening, together. And Barbara never said, "Why don't we go to yours for a change?" She didn't know why she didn't, and the only time she asked herself the question directly, she evaded, in reply, that it was too much trouble. It was an answer she made to a lot of her self-questioning. Too much trouble, too complicated, stop bothering me, she'd say when some inner compulsion forced her to ask why she would never assert herself, why she didn't have more friends, why, in spite of good marks, she didn't really get much pleasure from learning. The questions presented themselves, and you couldn't precisely ignore them, but Barbara had found a way to fob them off with *It's too much trouble, stop bothering me.*

But—and her mind went back to Katy—there's one thing to say for this relationship. I never *have* to be alone, the way some of the kids around school seem to have to be. I do have a lot of acquaintances, and I think I'll start trying to make friends with some of them, and then I won't really need Katy. Not that I wouldn't always like her, and be glad to be with her sometimes. I wouldn't need her. Put that way it didn't sound very elevating, but it was true. She supposed, without much concern, that lots of truths and some friendships were not very elevating. But you lived in the world on its terms, not on your own, and it was not a world of chivalry where Good went clothed in radiance and Evil bowed its head and asked forgiveness. It was, she thought, a world of personal uncertainty, of wars and class hatred and race hatred and anxiety and money worship, where Good still existed, but had better watch its step.

Andrew, coming upstairs to the kitchen, stopped and stared at his sister. "Hey, what's the matter with you?" he asked. "You look like you had glass eyes, or something."

"Hmm?" said Barbara. "Oh. Was I staring?"

"I don't know what you were doing, but it looked shivery."

"Sorry, darling. When's the show?"

"That's what I came up to tell everybody. We're ready. You wait here and I'll go get Dad and Mom, and then you can come down." He ran off, and Barbara waited obediently.

CHAPTER SIX

Andrew and Richard were prodigal of their time and gifts. It had taken a week, and heaven knew how much paint, composition and rehearsal, to get this show produced. It was over in fifteen minutes and they never gave another performance of this particular one.

What it is, Barbara decided, watching the drama of the jackal who trims a Christmas tree in order to lure a plump rooster into his home and, of course, learns to love his victim, what it is, is a real creative drive in these two. They like an audience for the final product, but it's the making of it that gives them pleasure. Like many a tale-teller, the boys had a strongly moral flavor to their story, which was simple enough. All animals should love and not eat each other. At the end of the second act nearly every puppet they owned had set up housekeeping with the regenerated jackal. The prediction was that they'd eat oatmeal and Hershey bars forever after. The curtain was rung down to an ovation, the producers came out from behind their puppet theater giggling and shoving each other, asking for ice cream.

"Wouldn't you think," Barbara said to her father a little later, "that they'd hate to have it all over so soon? I mean, they worked so hard, and it took such a little time. Wouldn't you think they'd want to talk about it, or do it over again tomorrow, or *something*?"

"The ways of those boys are passing strange," he agreed. "I don't think I would put that much time and effort into something so ephemeral. They didn't even make us clap very much. They could have wrung at least another minute out of me, anyway. And a couple more bravos, if they'd given me time."

"They really do seem to get their reward in the doing of things. You hear about that, but you practically never see it," Barbara mused.

"I don't know," her father said. "Wasn't your caroling last night rather on that order?"

No, it wasn't, Barbara thought. No matter what the rest of them did it for, I did it in order to be with them. She did not say this to her father. She said, instead, "Jeff's father is a nice man. Mr. Irwin."

Hal Perry nodded. "Good fellow."

"Oh? Do you know him?"

"Well, only from the drugstore, but he's always seemed a friendly kind."

"Did you know him when he came here last night?" she asked curiously.

"Of course I did. What makes you ask that?"

"I don't know." She paused, then went on. "Yes, I do. I mean that I didn't recognize him at all. And I've probably seen him as much as you have."

Her father didn't reply immediately. He seemed to turn her statement over in his mind before he said, "Why do you suppose that is?" He waited for her answer, waited quite unmistakably.

But Barbara could only mutter, "I don't know, Dad."

"You don't? Barbara, I think this is important. Do you really have no idea why you didn't recognize Mr. Irwin last night?"

She had an idea. Not a recognizable one. A sketch of an idea, the dimmest outline in a shadowy part of her mind. Nothing she could or would put into words. "No," she said dully. "None at all." She looked at her father sideways, through lowered lids, and he looked back at her steadily, as if he didn't believe this was her whole answer.

The phone rang. Relieved, slightly ruffled, Barbara went to answer it. He isn't fair, she thought—awkwardly, because that wasn't what she meant—it isn't fair, to come at me suddenly with questions that way, tempting me to think that if I made—found—an answer, things would begin to get clearer. Yet it was undermining, this feeling she got from him every now and then, that the solution to everything did not lie in the future, in a year not too far distant, when, simply through the chemistry of time, she would have found herself and the answers, too. Undermining to be forced to admit that there was never going to be a solution to everything, and that finding herself, or partial answers, wasn't going to just happen. The longer you put it off, his eyes on hers seemed to say, the harder it's going to be. And if you put it off too long, it may be too late.

He looked away as she picked up the phone, and Barbara repressed a sigh before she said, quite cheerfully, "Hello?"

"Hi, Barbara? This is Margaret Obemeyer—" Barbara's mouth opened a little in surprise, but Margaret was going on, "I'm calling everyone to thank them for coming last night and tell you we collected twenty-four dollars. Somebody put a five in, only I didn't notice who. But it was fun, wasn't it?"

"Oh, it was," Barbara said. "I liked it so much."

"I thought I'd never get unfrozen, but still—" Margaret's voice began to taper.

"Did you have a nice Christmas?" Barbara asked quickly.

"Oh, peachy. You?"

"Super." She hesitated, plunged on with a feeling of recklessness. "Say, Margaret, would you like—it just occurred to me—I mean, I have to stay in Friday night with my brothers and I wondered if you'd like to come over and spend the night . . . or just the evening, if you'd rather." She was breathing a little unsteadily, and her face was scarlet at her father's presence. Just as she thought this, he got up with a preoccupied air and went out of the room as if in search of something. Oh, he was . . . fastidious, all right. But he'd already heard her pleading. And he and Mother would just have to go out Friday night now, one way or another.

"Golly, I'm awfully sorry," Margaret was saying. Did she mean it? How could you tell if a person meant it when she said how sorry she was? *I* told Bud I was awfully sorry. "But I'm going to the movies with Bud Parker, Friday."

Barbara blinked at the phone, holding it away for a moment as if it had suddenly changed form. She put it cautiously back to her ear. "Bud Parker?" she said.

"Yes, he called and asked me this morning—" After he called me, Barbara was thinking. "—So I've already said yes. And anyway," Margaret went on, with that frankness of hers which was intended to be, and frequently was, disarming, "I'm just awfully pleased that he asked me. I mean, I'd definitely put him down as a misogynist—misanthrope—whatever that person is who hates women. Did you ever hear of him asking a girl out before?" Yes, me, thought Barbara. "So when he said 'movie,' I said 'Oh boy,' well, not really but practically. Well, but I'm awfully sorry about not seeing you. But maybe we can do it another time. Or you could come over here."

When she'd hung up, Barbara walked frowning to a chair, sat down to sort out her thoughts. Margaret had definitely sounded friendly, not at all surprised by her invitation for Friday. She'd sounded sincere about maybe making it another time, though she hadn't suggested any. She'd sounded . . . Barbara shook her head to clear it. Margaret Obemeyer was not only going out with Bud Parker, she was clearly, without reservation, delighted to be going. I don't understand, Barbara thought. She was puzzled and disheartened at this turn of events, as an opportunist is who has read the signs incorrectly. Bud was an outsider, wasn't he? He had never shown any sign of being eligible for this or any other school clique. Because he hadn't wished it? Was he a real example of what she took (she didn't know with how much sincerity) Katy to be . . . an outsider by choice? I should have said yes to him, she thought. I had that feeling, two or three times last night, of being drawn to him, but I resisted because—her mind stumbled but she went on doggedly, punishing herself—because I didn't think he was good enough. No, it wasn't that. Because I didn't think he'd do me any good where I most wanted it, with this particular crowd.

Her face was drawn, and her mind, in a series of useless repetitions, relived his phone call, and Margaret's.

PART TWO

CHAPTER ONE

"We're going out tonight," Mrs. Perry said to her husband after dinner on Friday night. They were lingering at the table. The children had gone to their rooms to do homework, Hector lay enormously stretched out on the floor, sighing every now and then in well-fed comfort. The night outside was black, starless, bitter cold. Mrs. Perry thought that to someone outside looking in it would be a homely, pleasant scene, this in their dining room. Glossy mahogany set with lacy mats, dishes bespeaking amplitude but not greed—she was not quite sure *how* a dish would bespeak this, but theirs did—a ham, nicely decorated and inexpertly carved (Hal apparently could not learn how), on a very old silver platter, Hector on the floor there—a powerful creature, very nearly a wolf, gentled by love and home and food. And the two of us,

she thought, Hal and I, perched on the brink of middle age, but not afraid, ready to flutter toward it together. "Like a pair of doves," she said aloud.

Her husband scowled at her. "Doves? I got the part about going out, and let me tell you I disapprove. In principle, in practice, I disapprove of our having to go out because Barbara tells social lies, and I'm not at all sure that I'll go. What have doves got to do with it?"

"You and I, dear, are like a pair of brave doves, perched on the brink of middle age, ready to flutter toward it together."

His scowl became a stare of dismay. "Listen . . . even in fun, don't talk that way. You have no idea what it does to my digestion." He rubbed his chin. "I don't want to go out tonight. I'd have to shave." Mrs. Perry said nothing. "Letty, do you think yourself that there's anything rational or ethical in her being able to drive us out of the house this way?"

"Oh well . . . drive?" she protested softly.

"Yes. Drive. I don't want to go out. Do you want to go out?" His wife hesitated, shrugged. "The point is, doesn't she have to learn that she can't dispose of people, willy-nilly, simply in order to convert her lies to truths?"

"Hal, what she did wasn't lying. You do much the same sort of thing yourself. We all do. Only no one can call us to account for it."

"In a way." He subsided, started up again. "Still, I think she should be made to understand—"

"She will," Letty Perry said pacifically. "You'll see to it."

"What *is* she going to do tonight?"

"Katy Stryker is coming over."

"You know, that girl reminds me of someone. I think it's Carmen. Sort of fateful."

"Faithful?"

"*Fate*ful. Fraught with destiny. And not a good one."

"Why do you say that?"

"Oh, I don't suppose I really believe it. It's just an impression she gives—means to give, too. All that black hair and white skin, and the gestures. Her arms are like veils in a prophesying wind."

"She's fifteen. Remember what Dr. Palmer said."

"Still, it's difficult to tell where hormones leave off and character begins. If we're going out, I'd better shave. Where are we going, by the way?"

"Anne Weber phoned this afternoon and wanted to know if we wanted to go over there tonight. So, you see, we had an invitation after all."

"Which doesn't affect the basic situation."

"No. Go and shave. I'll get the table cleared."

Still he didn't go. "What are the Strykers like?" he asked. "Do you know them?"

"Not well. He's a salesman for some patent medicine. On the road a lot, I guess. And she's . . . just a woman. I used to see her at P.T.A. meetings when Katy and Barbara were in grammar school. I still see her once in a while, and talk to her on the phone occasionally. She complains a lot."

"About what?"

"Oh, anything. You know. A habit, more than anything else, I guess. She told me once, a long time ago, that life was just a series of disillusions. But lots of people say that."

"Only idealists."

"How do you mean?"

"It's the idealists who end up without illusions. They fall too far short of their goals too often. They're always having to compromise, always being disappointed—and disappointing. I'm glad I'm a realist."

"You weren't during the war. At least, you used to write what I'd consider pretty idealistic letters."

"War's different. You have to look at ideals then, because you *can't* open your eyes and look at reality. What you see is too unbelievable, and realists have to believe in what they see."

"Only? Entirely?"

"No, not only or entirely. But one of the basics of realism is the *wish* to look at things as they are. I couldn't do that during the war. I didn't believe a thing I saw all the time I was overseas, so naturally I had to strike out for idealism. There wasn't any reality."

"In a way," Letty Perry said, "that may be what the children Barbara's age are doing. Waving idealism around like a flag, because they just aren't ready for reality yet. Sometimes I try to remember how I felt, and, believe me, I was the battleground for a civil war. Right within myself." She folded her napkin carefully, put it beside her plate. "You get to that age, and there's part of you wanting to secede from childhood and parents and all the things that represent slavery to you, and there's the other part scared to death of secession and only wanting everything to stay unchanged. And there are you, not only providing the battleground, but the ammunition and the war cries and the armies for both sides. It's a wonder there aren't more casualties, instead of the few we complain about." She laughed a little. "End of speech. Go and *shave*."

Her husband turned at the door. "It was a good speech, nonetheless."

When he'd gone, Mrs. Perry cleared the table, walking slowly between dining room and kitchen, her face preoccupied. A good speech, and true, in a way. But you never could tell how well you remembered your feelings, nor, for that matter, how your feelings—well or ill remembered—applied to young people today. Human emotions didn't change very much, did they? Or was that one of the things people said in order not to have to give much thought to human problems? Weren't young people today far more sophisticated, more knowing, more embittered (thus, perhaps, according to Hal, more idealistic?) than young people of her day had been? We had a depression, and the feeling of unease over the world, but we didn't actually know or believe there was another world war coming until Hitler started to march. Today all the young people seem to expect . . . No, she couldn't say it. She couldn't believe it, because the next one would be the end of everything. Of course, they'd said that about the last one, too. But with the things that had been built and discovered since the last one . . . the incomprehensible destructiveness that had been harnessed but could so easily be let loose . . . there could be no survival of life as they now knew it.

Some people said that life as they now knew it was not worth surviving for, that it would be better for humanity to finish itself off and let some new experiment begin its millions-of-years climb out of the mud toward some different, better goal. Nothing in Letty Perry responded to that. People were, in her mind, incredible, magnificent. Oh, perhaps not individuals here and there, perhaps not certain sections of human history, but the experiment of mankind was not a thing to be scrapped because all aspects of the experiment had not come up to expectation. There was time . . . there was time for all the growth and flowering and moving toward perfection that any great enterprise could require, if only some few small fractions of it were not allowed to bring annihilation on the whole. When she thought these things, panic began to dash within her like a maddened insect in a bottle. She had to stop and, quite literally, take deep breaths to steady herself.

It isn't, she thought now, turning off the dining-room light, solely the personal terror of a mother with two sons. It's deeper than that, I'm sure it is. It's the anguish that anyone who nurtures or creates—a parent, a gardener, a painter—must feel when the lovingly tended work is threatened, when it seems that all that has gone into its fabric—the hardiness, the sensibility, the color, the balance, the *heart*—may be destroyed with little more than a gesture.

But young people, she thought, forcing her mind back a bit, young people today seem to expect the worst, but hope for the best, and that's probably the ultimate realism for our time.

As she started upstairs to say good night to her children, she realized that within ten minutes she had moved from youth which carried idealism aloft like a banner to youth which had arrived at the terminus of realism, and all of it in what had seemed a perfectly logical sequence. The person I bless, she told herself, is that man who called consistency the hobgoblin of little minds. How much confusion and self-doubt has he spared me, and at the same time given me a fine great mind untenanted by hobgoblins. I think consistent people are sort of lifeless, anyway.

She rapped lightly on her daughter's door. "Barbara?"

"Come in."

Barbara was at her desk. Slim legs wrapped around the chair legs, left hand clutching her hair, she leaned over her homework with an air of chilly competence. "Just a sec," she said, scribbled a moment longer, then turned to her mother. "All done."

Isn't it a pity you can't take some pleasure in it, Mrs. Perry thought, but refrained from uttering the words. Once begin voicing your unspoken thoughts along *that* line and life would be nothing but a series of helpful hints reproachfully uttered. Isn't it a pity you don't like your homework, your Aunt Edna, your nice fried fish. Barbara did her homework, was polite to Aunt Edna when she saw her, which wasn't often, and fixed herself an egg in place of fish. Any of these attitudes might change in time, but not through persuasion, and meanwhile there were always so many things you *had* to say.

"Has Katy decided yet whether she's going to spend the night?"

Barbara shook her head. "She never decides anything until the last minute."

"Well, but do be sure to tell her that if she isn't going to, why your father will drive her home tonight. And, Barbara, we won't be in too late, and your father will want her to go *then*."

"What's not too late?"

"We should be back by midnight."

"Then she'll have to stay. We . . . you barely get talking by midnight."

Mrs. Perry began a protest, let it die. It was true. When you had a friend in, you barely got talking by midnight. She didn't think Barbara was terribly close to Katy, but there again was a thing you could not mention or inquire about. The privacy of a girl of fifteen, she thought now, is better guarded than an atomic pile.

"Well, you and Katy do what you wish, but I'd certainly think you'd let her mother know what you've decided well before midnight. And we'll be home by then."

"We will," Barbara said impatiently, and then suddenly, impulsively, got up and threw her arms briefly around her mother's neck, drew away again and smiled. It was the sweet, unself-conscious smile she had had as a child, and was gone before Mrs. Perry had time to more than recognize it.

"I . . ." She didn't know what to say. Her hand went to her hair in a woman's uncertain gesture. "That was nice."

"For free," Barbara said. "I just suddenly thought how nice you are." As if the moment were now too much for her, she turned away. "You and I say *nice* too much."

"Better than divine," Mrs. Perry said.

She stood in the doorway, reluctant to leave, aware that she should, that pointless lingering only took the unexpected moment further into the domain of strangeness.

"Have a nice evening," she said, and went down the hall. If I were a writer I would write about these sudden, unlooked-for moments of closeness, not just between parent and child but between any human beings. Sometimes between strangers this look of ageless understanding is exchanged. The eyes meet in a moment formal and profound, something is given, something taken, before each of you goes his way. I've known such an interchange once or twice, and if I were a poet might, because they can never be other than caught in flight, find them richer than moments such as Barbara and I just knew, the like of which we have known in the past, and will surely know again in the future. But I am a mother, and do not envy poets their riches.

The walls of the boys' room were hung with animal pictures and a large beautiful map of Africa which they'd gotten for Christmas. Richard, when his mother came in the room, was sitting cross-legged on his bed, studying the map. He leaned forward a little, then turned to include her in his survey.

"This has got everything," he said appreciatively. "All these little trees, and monkeys and lions and camels." He shook his head. "Camels have an awful funny dumb look about them, come to think of it." Richard had a way of putting phrases like "come to think of it," or "taken all in all," in his conversation. They were imitative of his father, sounded a bit pedantic and rather amazed people who didn't know him well.

"Come to think of it, they do," Mrs. Perry said. "Sort of silly and haughty."

"Down here's crocodiles," Richard said, becoming absorbed.

Mrs. Perry moved to Andrew's side. He was at the desk, writing in the front of a book with a pencil stub not more than an inch long. His tongue was caught in the corner of his mouth, with the toe of one sneaker he kicked the heel of the other repeatedly, and the fingers of his left hand tormented his ear lobe. The chair was pushed so far back that he had to sit on the very edge and strain forward in order to reach the desk at all.

"Comfortable?" said his mother.

Andrew glanced up, grinned and nodded. "Look," he said, waving at the book. "In case it ever gets lost."

Mrs. Perry looked, and was not surprised to find:

Andrew Joseph Perry
11 Carmel Ave
Nortown, Ohio
United States of America
North America
Western Hemisphere
The Earth
The Solar System
The Universe

"That should get it back to you," she smiled. And then, because the boys were still at the age when the fact of their own parents' childhood rather fascinated them, she said, "I used to do that, too."

"Did you?" said Andrew with pleasure. "Just like I did?"

"I can't remember, really. I guess maybe I left the solar system out." He looked dubious, so she added, "I never lost the book anyway."

"You and Dad going out tonight?" he asked.

"Yes."

"Where?"

"To the Webers'."

"Is Barby sitting with us?"

"Yes. Her friend Katy is coming over to be with her."

Andrew nodded. "You know Katy's adopted?" His mother's eyes widened, and he shrugged a little, disclaiming responsibility for the Strykers' choice. "Yup. Not Fay, though. Her little sister. She says Fay is her parents' child. Katy doesn't see how a person could get as obnoxious as Fay in only ten years."

Mrs. Perry couldn't decide what to say. She settled for, "Do you think you should eavesdrop, Andrew?" Was there any point in telling him that Katy was not adopted? Better tell him not to repeat it, anyway.

"I wasn't eavesdropping," Andrew said unconcernedly. "They just talk as if we couldn't hear. Or maybe—" he slid a smile up at her "—as if we couldn't understand. Lots of people think you can't understand anything if you aren't as old as they are."

Mrs. Perry had to agree with that. "But don't . . . don't go around saying Katy's adopted, will you, dear?"

"Why should I? Who cares?"

"Well . . . it isn't that."

What were the ethics in this thing? Did she tell Andrew Katy was imagining things? It would not deceive Andrew, who would translate it into "Katy's a liar." You wouldn't want to call the girl a liar. Even if she is one, Mrs. Perry thought, then rebuked herself and decided probably it was just Katy's spirited imagination. On the other hand, it was a sort of unpleasant thing to imagine.

Andrew by now had forgotten Katy and was over at the map. "Look here," he said to his mother. "Did you see the whales down in the corner, spouting?"

Mrs. Perry, joining them, decided to let the matter of Katy's parentage drop. But later on, in the car, she said to her husband, "Did you know Katy Stryker goes around saying she's adopted?"

"Is she?"

"Hal . . . she was born a month after Barbara. In the same hospital. I went to visit and took some booties that someone had given me."

"Sounds conclusive. How in the world you remember these things is—"

"Do you think she should go around saying such a thing?"

"I don't suppose anyone would pay much attention. What do you propose to do about it, anyway?"

"Nothing. It's just—" She stopped, stared at the road

illumined by their headlights. "I hope *Barbara* doesn't say—or think—such a thing."

"Oh, I doubt if it's contagious. Anyway, it isn't a phenomenon, you know. Loads of kids go through the I'm-adopted phase. No harm done, really."

Sometimes, Mrs. Perry thought, I really think there's no such thing as an understanding man. Callous and indifferent, the lot of them, and I get sick of it. She hunched in her coat, refusing to talk, impatiently aware that Hal, who could go for hours in silence, did not know that he was being punished.

CHAPTER TWO

Katy was the most restless person that Barbara had ever known. It seemed she almost literally couldn't relax, remain in one position for more than a minute, or even, until the evening had considerably advanced, remain in one room. She wandered from kitchen to living room to dining room, fiddling with the phonograph, the draperies, the centerpiece (which toppled over when she touched it and could not be induced to go back in order again). She ran her fingers lightly through her hair (so that it always had a slightly uncombed look that was not unattractive), along the ridged edge of a chair cover, around the rim of an ash tray. And when Katy was there they always put a stack of records on because a background of silence was unendurable to her.

"Do you do this when you're at home, too?" Barbara asked.

"Do what?"

"Prowl. I'd prowl too, you know, to keep you company, but it's sort of tiring."

Katy dropped into a chair, caught a lock of hair and twisted it. "I get—" she tossed one hand, as if she wanted to throw it away "—wriggly. I don't know what it is. Some sort of neurosis, maybe. Yes, sort of as if, if I sat still —and especially if I sat still in silence—something would catch up with me, or I'd hear something I'd rather not hear."

"Like what?"

"Well, I don't know," Katy said dryly. "That's the whole point. I don't know and I don't intend to find out, so I have to keep running around and playing the radio . . . I put the radio on as soon as I get in my room, and it doesn't go off till I fall asleep and it wakes me up in the morning. One of those alarm clock radios."

"You study with it on?"

"I couldn't study with it off."

"I tried that. It didn't work."

Katy was uninterested in Barbara's study habits. "No, but you have no idea what it's like, being so high-strung. Sometimes I think I'll go crazy. And other times, when I'm walking home from school or something, I'll decide just to keep walking. One day I'll walk past the house and keep walking and *never* come back."

"Where would you go?"

"Barbara, do you have to be so literal? I don't know,

and I don't care. Just away." She got up and walked to the window, where she stood staring out. "Just away."

I wonder why we bother with each other? Barbara thought. She thinks I'm stodgy, and I think she's hysterical, and we really have nothing to say to each other. Is it the same old business of not wanting to be without some security? As long as we're friends—if you could call us that—as long as we assume this guise of friendship, we don't have to worry about being that most desperate of figures—the isolated teen-ager. She looked at Katy's slender, nervous figure, vacillating at the window. Why did I think she was lonely through choice? Nobody's lonely through choice, and I'll bet she's even lonelier than I am, because at least I know who my parents are. Of course, Katy does, too, but it would be lonely even to pretend that you didn't.

"Do you really believe that you're adopted?" she said suddenly.

"What?" Katy was twisting the cord of the Venetian blind and didn't turn around.

"I said do you really believe that you're adopted."

Katy lifted her shoulders and let them drop. "There goes Ellen Murray, off to the movies with her lord and master. Does she go out with him every night?"

"Practically."

Katy returned to her chair. "Gee, she's a fool."

"I agree. Maybe she's in love with him, though."

"In *love.* Girls who get married right out of high school are doing it to get away from home."

"There are other ways to get away from home."

"Getting married's the easiest."

Barbara didn't think she agreed with that. "Suppose nobody asked you?"

Katy turned her beautiful head to study Barbara thoughtfully. "You know, it's that sort of attitude that leads to saying yes to the first person who asks you. I'll bet the world is full of people who are married for no other reason except that the girl didn't think anyone else would ask her. And if you ask me, you'd still be better off, if no one else ever *did,* than going and getting yourself married, just so you'll be."

"Be what?"

"Married, married," Katy said impatiently.

"Well, I certainly hope I get married someday," Barbara said, and felt at once that she'd missed the point.

Katy got up and walked into the dining room, tried to get the French heather to stand up. "I'm sorry about this," she said. "But it's awfully dry or something."

"It's all right, I told you."

"Well, but I wouldn't want your mother to be annoyed."

"Mother doesn't get annoyed about things like that," Barbara said. "Look, can't you come in here and sit down? And stay down? When do you do all this lying around that you're supposed to do at home?"

Katy came back, laughing a little. "At home I'm thinking."

"About what?"

"How to get away from home, of course."

For a while they were silent. They listened to a crooner, Katy twisting her hair and brooding, Barbara wishing she hadn't asked her and hoping she wouldn't decide to stay all night. Every now and then Katy seemed to think so clearly, but in the end she just complained. A couple of malcontents, Barbara thought, egging each other on. And I'm beginning to get tired of it.

She felt vaguely oppressed and, at the same time, distantly stirred by a feeling that somehow life was going to be different. *I'm* going to be different, she thought. But she didn't know in what way, or even how to begin thinking about it so long as Katy was here. I wish I had the nerve to ask her to go home. I wish I could say, "Katy, you and I only make each other uncomfortable, we're only together now because neither of us knew what other use to make of this evening, so why don't we part?" But you didn't say such things. Not if you'd been properly brought up. Not, she thought, if you'd never in your life been honest with anyone, except the members of your family once in a while. Oh, you can honestly say a pleasant thing . . . but did people ever say, not in unkindness but just in simple truth, I prefer not to be with you, and I know you prefer not to be with me? She supposed not. Children could be frank and take frankness for granted, but once you left childhood you were trapped in this pattern of politeness. And it's even worse for people like me, she thought, who are so . . . so darned *servile*. In an access of thwartedness, she glared at Katy, who stared blandly back.

"What's your trouble?" Katy asked.

"Trouble?" Barbara said in confusion. "What do you mean?"

"You were looking at me as if I'd discovered your secret and posted it on the bulletin board."

"No, I wasn't. I mean . . . I don't know what I mean. I'm in a sort of bad mood tonight, maybe. I wonder," she said slowly, "if Margaret Obemeyer ever gets in a bad mood. I suppose she does, but you'd never know it."

"Everybody's dream girl."

You're jealous, Barbara thought. "Why do you say that?"

Katy didn't answer for a moment. Then she tipped her chin up a little, as one preparing for an argument, and said, "Anyone who's that popular with everybody has something wrong with her. It stands to reason, doesn't it? Everyone *can't* like the same kind of person, so someone everybody likes is being . . . being different according to who she meets. One man's Margaret and another man's Mitzi."

Barbara realized she wasn't going to answer. She was

not going to stick up for Margaret, stand up to Katy, she was neither going to agree nor disagree. She was going to smile the nervous smile that always forced its way to her lips when she was faced with the risk of alienating someone—anyone.

My trouble, she thought desperately, is that I want to be liked by everybody, the way Margaret is, only I don't know how to go about it, except by conciliating. Margaret doesn't conciliate. And I *know* she doesn't betray herself and anyone who doesn't happen to be around in this constant effort to achieve a place of affection in which to be secure. There's really something the matter with me. Maybe I ought to go see a doctor, or a minister. Maybe—the thought came quite unbidden—I should talk to my father. She turned away from the idea, not asking herself why.

"We're supposed to call your mother," she said, "and let her know if you're staying all night."

"That sounds suspiciously like a hint."

"No, it isn't. Only we are supposed to. Have you decided yet?"

Katy raked her fingers through her black hair. "I'm going home. I have to get up early and study. I have to get straight A's this year or they won't let me keep on carrying five subjects."

"Why do you want to, anyway?"

"Because if I don't I won't get all the science courses I want."

I didn't know she wanted any, Barbara thought. "What do you want them for?"

"I'm going to be a doctor."

Barbara stiffened. How could she make such a positive statement? She could say she wanted to be, or hoped to be. . . . "How can you say definitely what you want to be in the tenth grade? There are all sorts of things—"

"Not for me," Katy said. "I knew years ago."

"You never told me."

"You never asked. Actually, of course, you didn't ask now, I just told you. But you never do ask people what they're interested in."

"Have you ever asked me?" Barbara asked, with a faint tartness.

Katy looked honestly surprised. "Well, sure I have. You're going to be a writer and an actress and a lawyer and a ballet dancer and—" She broke off. "Don't look so peevish, Barbara. I think it's great to want to be all those things, and you have plenty of time to decide. I'm only saying that I decided years ago and never changed my mind."

Barbara, put out at being called peevish, did not reply, and Katy got up and went to phone her mother. "Hello . . . oh, Fay, it's you. Well, tell Mother I'll be home about—" She cupped the phone, said to Barbara, "How am I getting home?"

"My father's driving you. They said they'd be home by

midnight." It seemed much too far away, but there was nothing to do about it.

Katy delivered this message to her sister and hung up. "Gee, that Fay is a pill."

Do you ever say anything nice about anyone? Barbara wondered. "She's pretty."

"I suppose so. But she never lets me have any privacy. In fact, nobody in that house has any privacy, only it appears I'm the only one who cares. I don't even ask people over, not even you, because we'd never have a minute alone."

"Is that really so?" Barbara asked, surprised.

"Sure, it's so. I've told them a million times that people with manners knock on a door before they come in. But they think people with manners don't close doors. We just don't understand each other in that house. Not the least bit."

"What do they think about your idea of being a doctor?"

"It isn't an idea, it's a decision. They don't believe me. But it doesn't matter. I'm going to have to get scholarships and work my way through anyway. I think my father could afford to put me through premed, but I don't think he's about to do it, so—" Her eyes moved restlessly. "What are your brothers doing?"

"Reading, I suppose." Barbara looked at her watch. "It's past ten. I'd better go up and see that they get to bed."

But Richard and Andrew had gotten themselves to bed. They were propped against pillows, reading, and assured her that their teeth and hands were washed.

"Well, you'd better go to sleep now," Barbara said. She opened the window a little, looked around the room and then said impulsively, "Do you think I'm interested in what you're doing?"

Richard glanced up from his book, decided this question was quite out of his range, returned to Blackie Crow without a word. But Andrew said willingly enough, "Interested in what we're doing when?"

"Any time," Barbara said, feeling slightly foolish. Still, Andrew *was* in the frank period, and he often showed extreme perception about people. She could do worse than look to him for an answer—part of an answer—to her problems.

"Well," he said cautiously, "you like our puppet shows."

"But what?" Barbara persisted. Reservation was written all over him.

"Maybe you'll be different when you're older," he said, looking at her with alert, interested eyes. "When you're a parent or something."

"Different from what?" Barbara cried.

"Well, from how you are now. Sort of sad and selfish," he concluded patly.

Those aren't his own words, Barbara thought. Where

did he hear them? Cold, even a little frightened, she said, "Who said that about me, Andrew?"

He shook his head. "I don't remember, Barby. But I expect they're right. Anyway, you do have this sort of sad look most of the time."

This is awful, Barbara thought. Simply awful. As if she were compelled to, she said, "And the selfish part?"

"What do you mean?" His eyes strayed to his book. He was obviously beginning not to like the conversation, but Barbara wouldn't let him off so easily.

"Do you think I'm selfish?" she said, and held his glance a moment longer.

Andrew wavered, turned, and made a full retreat into childhood, where he knew perfectly well she couldn't follow him. "You do give us things sometimes," he said obtusely.

Abruptly tired from the whole evening, Barbara said good night to them. "Don't read any more," she said. "It's past your bedtime now."

She closed their door and went downstairs, wondering how in the world she'd last till midnight. I have to get alone and think. I have to—now, let's see—if I take this slowly, step by step, maybe I can make some sense out of these last few days. Because somehow it seemed that in the past days her life had become tangled and unmanageable, like thread going wild on a bobbin. It wasn't really in the last few days, of course. This had been coming on for a couple of years or more, but the confusion was suddenly so *clear* (which didn't make sense either, but at this point absolutely nothing was making any sense) that there simply was no possibility of continuing to ignore it. Now, let's see. . . .

But she couldn't think yet. There was still Katy, and a couple of hours to be gotten through. "Let's look at the television," she said when she got downstairs.

Katy, after the longest yawn Barbara had ever seen, agreed.

CHAPTER THREE

And then, to her astonishment, Margaret called the next morning. Mr. Perry answered the telephone. She heard him say, "Hello? Oh, hello, Margaret. How are you?" He didn't know Margaret, but wasn't sure that he didn't, and in any case always went out of his way to be polite to Barbara's friends. "Me? Oh, I'm tired. . . . No, no, not sick. I just believe in being tired on Saturday. . . . One second, I'll get Barbara for you—"

Barbara was already at his side. He handed the phone over, and went in search of his wife, who proved to be in the laundry room downstairs. "Did you ever phone about having that extension put in?" he asked.

Mrs. Perry closed her eyes, opened them and looked at him helplessly. "I can't think what's wrong with me, Hal.

I've got it written down on about six bits of paper here and there, and I *keep* forgetting."

"You needn't be a student of Freud to figure that one out," her husband said, and then, to change the subject, "I'm going to get all your bits of paper together and put out a book. *The Collected Scribbles of Letitia Perry.* How does that sound?"

"What did you mean by that?"

He debated whether to misunderstand, decided not to. "I mean that you're edgy with Barbara lately, and really you can't be blamed, but unconsciously you're denying her the telephone, as a sort of punishment."

"That's pretty glib."

"I could be wrong," he said, with no indication of thinking he was.

"Do-it-yourself home psychiatry," she muttered, pulling clothes from the drier, sorting the things that must be ironed from those she could not possibly avoid ironing.

"I said I could be wrong."

"Yes, but you probably aren't." She folded a sheet, held it against her, and looked at him rather dreamily. "Do you remember, when we were young, how angry you used to make me with your pronouncements that nearly always turned out to be right? Like the time I was so wild about that boy who was going to be a herpetologist?"

"Oh, that fellow," Hal said, with a faint grin. "What a host of tiresome memories the thought of him recalls."

"And I said you were just frittering away your time,

and at least he was a specialist, and you said a specialist is somebody who doesn't do anything else well, and that's just how it turned out. He couldn't dance, or carry on a conversation . . . all he did was talk about snakes." She smiled at her husband. "You did put up with a lot."

"I still do," he assured her. "Besides, I don't like that way you have of saying, When we were young. I don't know about you, but I'm not forty, and I am not yet prepared for a wheel chair and wistful recollections of the past."

"I only meant in comparison with Barbara. You *must* remember that. When you're in your teens, anyone in their twenties is pretty advanced, and further than that—" she frowned, trying to recollect "—why, my goodness, further than that, you not only don't have any emotions, it would be positively indecent if you did."

"You'll forgive me if I don't order my life in accordance with a fifteen-year-old's picture of what it should be."

"Oh, there isn't any way to please them, or heaven knows I'd do—I really do do—what I can to please Barbara. We both do. But I really think sometimes that no matter which way you work it, you turn out wrong, because you *are* a parent. You and I behave ourselves, the Strykers fight all the time, the Lawsons scarcely speak to each other, and the Frosts are still acting like a honeymoon couple, but I can't see that any of the children involved vary in their attitudes toward us."

"You can't really know."

"No, but I talk to them—the Frosts and Strykers and all—and I've been in their homes when the children were, and it all seems the same to me. A sort of . . . watchfulness. As if they were waiting for us to misunderstand, or do something wrong, or hurt their feelings. And yet—it's a funny thing, Hal—they're so . . . so appealing at that age." She thought, but wouldn't put into words, that they, the young people she knew, like Barbara and Jeff and Katy, were like certain young animals, calves or deer, balanced on the edge of poise, foolish and lovely and unapproachable. Did I really forget the telephone deliberately? "I'm going up now and phone about that extension," she said.

"Well, I might as well work, I suppose."

"Isn't it going well, dear?" she asked.

Hal Perry looked uncomfortable. "You sound like Jane Carlyle inquiring as to the progress of the *French Revolution*. This is a sixth-grade history text."

"I realize that," she said stiffly. "Can't I ask about it?"

"Not in that tone," he insisted. "Not as if it were a Work in Progress."

Annoyed with his irritation, Letty went upstairs without waiting to see if he followed. He's bored by that book, she thought. Why doesn't he just drop it? But, of course, he could not. You grow older, and the time when there are any number of choices falls away almost without your noticing (and, no matter what Hal said, their own youth was now legend) and you are left inescapably to finish the sixth-grade textbook. Once it had not seemed impossible to Hal that he should be another Carlyle. Once I was Shaw's *Cleopatra* before a high-school audience, and dreamed of being Shakespeare's before a Broadway one. Now I dream of making a better flower arrangement than Anne Weber does—and never will, of course.

"What a giddy standard," she said to Barbara, as they met in the hall.

"Whose?"

Mrs. Perry wondered whether she had the breath or the interest to explain, realized she did not, and shook her head. "Just talking to myself. Darling, I'm going to telephone about that extension, this minute."

"That's nice," Barbara said in a reserved voice. Mrs. Perry heard reproach in it.

"For heaven's sake, Barbara, I'm sorry I didn't do it sooner. But you know how things keep coming up, and I *have* meant to, at least a dozen times. I have it written on all sorts of slips of paper—"

"Why are you yelling at me? I didn't say anything."

"I'm not yelling. I never yell."

"Maybe it'd be better if you did."

She isn't being rude, Letty Perry said to herself. And anyway, I started it. But what in the world is the matter between Barbara and me? Like a pair of cats, forced to share the same dish, we eye each other and tuck our whiskers back and arch our backs a little, and that's all it ever comes to. Maybe she's right, maybe it'd be better if we put out our claws and let fly at each other. But everything she'd ever believed resisted the picture of an open battle with a child. Barbara isn't a child any more, something within her said. She is almost a woman. Was that, then, the trouble? The ancient enmity of two women beneath the same roof?

Oh, I don't believe it, she thought, brushing a nervous hand through her hair, and feeling horribly on the verge of tears. Not alone for Barbara and this impassable void between them. For everything, she thought, sad beyond definitions. I could weep for everything.

"Anyway," she said, on a deep breath, "you could have called them yourself."

"Yes," Barbara said slowly. "Funny, though. I didn't think of it. I suppose I was just waiting for you to."

And you don't, Mrs. Perry thought, need to be a student of Freud to figure that out. She reached for the telephone, asked for the business office and got an extremely pleasant woman to whom she was presently explaining the need of an extension in their rumpus room. ". . . for my daughter," she said, "so she won't have to talk in front of all of us, and heaven knows I don't blame her."

"Neither do I," said the telephone representative. "I had to get one for my son. It's in a coat closet, of all places, and I suppose he'll suffocate one day, but that's where he wanted it."

"Aren't they marvelous?" Letty Perry laughed.

"Oh, they are. I go almost crazy, but I think they're marvelous. How many do you have?"

"Three. That is, my two sons are much younger and wouldn't mind if the telephone were on the lawn, but their day will come. How many do you have?"

"Just the one son, but he feels like a half a dozen."

Barbara leaned against the wall, shaking her head. Mother just cannot help enjoying things. For a second there she really looked as if she'd cry, and it was awful and I nearly wanted to put my arms around her, and now look.

In the summertime, in their garden, the Perrys had seven tall sunflowers. Barbara was pretty sure they were eight feet high, or perhaps more. They had enormous yellow heads with dark dusty eyes, wide ragged leaves, and they stood in a row like seven women engaged in conversation and slowly turned sunward as the day progressed. Barbara thought of them now. Mother is like that. A sunflower woman, nodding and conversing and following the sun, and no more able not to respond to the breeze and the light than the sunflowers are. Waiting for her to finish on the telephone, Barbara thought about the way her mother could be deflected from annoyance, even from sadness, just by a word, from a friend or a stranger. It's almost as if she were superficial, and yet she really isn't. There is something very steady in my mother, very strong, and how does that fit in with her absolute inability to dislike anybody, to remain angry or unhappy? *Any-body* can make friends with my mother, and even that time when Richard was so sick, I caught her in the hospital discussing African violets with a nurse, and as if she really *cared*.

Barbara remembered that time very well. She'd come up in the elevator and along the hall to Richard's room, and just outside the door her mother and this nurse had stood talking.

"Well, what I do," her mother was saying, "and it isn't my own idea—somebody told me—is use the water that you boil for tea, after it's gotten cool, of course, and put it in the saucer. Never pour it over the plant. At least, that's what I'm told, and I must say mine do pretty well, considering how unreliable an African violet is."

"I'll certainly try it," the nurse had said. "Poor thing needs some sort of treatment other than what I've been giving it." She'd turned to see Barbara. "Now, here's your daughter, Mrs. Perry. I must be getting on." She'd given that look of special pleasure that Mrs. Perry seemed to summon up, and had gone on down the hall.

"Mother," Barbara had said tensely, "how can you stand around talking about flowers, with Richard lying in there so sick? How can you?"

For a moment it seemed as if Mrs. Perry might not answer. Then she said, "She's a woman who lives alone, and she's been doing floor duty for forty years. Somebody gave her a plant and she wanted to talk about it." Searching Barbara's face, she'd waited, but Barbara had had nothing to say.

Now, listening to her mother discuss the telephone operator's son's acne, she stirred restlessly, but something in the deepest, most honest part of her mind relented and said, "This woman, and whether she's my mother or not has nothing to do with it, is genuinely loving. It must be very rare." The thought was something whole, but immediately eclipsed, like a landscape in a lightning flash.

"Mother, for heaven's sake," she whispered urgently.

Mrs. Perry said a word or two more, hung up. "We just got talking."

"You always just get talking," Barbara said, adding at once, "And I don't understand it."

"There's nothing to understand."

Barbara rejected this statement, but, since she didn't want to talk about her mother but about herself, allowed it to pass. "Margaret Obemeyer invited me to a party tonight," she said casually.

"Why, darling, how *lovely*," Mrs. Perry said, and then, as if sensing too much enthusiasm in her tone, went on with indifference, "Are you going?"

"Oh, *Mother*," Barbara giggled. "Of course I'm going. It's all right to act pleased."

"Difficult to be sure," her mother murmured. "Remember me to Mrs. Obemeyer."

"Do you know her?"

"Oh, yes. She's the chairman of everything."

She herself was never chairman of anything, mainly through terror of having to get up in front of a group of people and talk. Hal diagnosed that as self-concern and she didn't care what he called it, so long as she didn't have to do it. "Did I ever tell you," she said to Barbara now, forgetting her own rule of not referring to her past with her daughter, "that I once acted Cleopatra? In high school?"

"You did?" Barbara said in amazement.

"Yes," said Mrs. Perry, amazed in turn that Barbara hadn't immediately changed the subject. "I did. And I loved it, and then all of a sudden I couldn't even talk up in a class. I had my brief moment, and the rest has been silence. Well, not to say silence, I talk enough certainly. But I get all unglued at the idea of talking in *front* of people. Do you know," she frowned, "that when I was in college, I told every professor, at the beginning of each year, not to call on me in class because I wouldn't answer?"

"I certainly didn't know it," Barbara said, interested in spite of herself—she really did not like to have her mother reminisce. "Did you get away with it?"

"Yes. I suppose because they didn't actually care if I spoke or not. I sometimes think they didn't even care if we learned anything. I could be wrong, of course. But when you go to college, I hope you pick one that doesn't have such enormous classes."

"I'll probably go to Dad's, won't I?"

"Oh *no*," her mother protested. "We never said you should go there. That's just a mill."

"Then why does Dad teach there?"

Mrs. Perry sighed. "Why, indeed? Because, I suppose, it's where he happens to teach, and if there's a better answer we haven't found it. You get into a rut, thinking it's just for a moment, that pretty soon you'll get out and go on to something new . . . and the first thing you know the rut is so deep you can never climb out."

No, Barbara thought, no, I don't want to hear about it. I don't want to glimpse any part of what's bleak in your mind, or sad. I don't want to know about your disappointments and Dad's failures. Those are yours, and I don't want to know about them—

"What are you going to wear tonight?" her mother said, on such a warm, bright note that Barbara, suspicious for a moment, relaxed. She had, after all, only imagined wistfulness or disillusion in her mother's voice. Her mother was a good-humored, happy person, almost recklessly optimistic, and you wouldn't have her any other way. What it came to was you *couldn't*.

"My navy wool, don't you think?"

"Yes. The navy wool would be perfect."

They looked at each other for a long moment, intensely aware of much else that could be said—*How did she happen to ask you, darling, and do tell me that it's made you happy, let's share it. Mother, it's like a dream come true, I am bursting with happiness and terror because this is surely a turning point in my life.*

They struggled a moment, whether to give in or to resist, Barbara wasn't sure, but then Andrew came by, and time had paid out that moment forever.

"I don't suppose," he said to his sister, "you want to help us build a snowman." He scarcely made it a question.

"Yes," said Barbara quickly. Yes, anything at all. But as she turned to go upstairs and dress for a snowman, she gave her mother a smile in which she tried to put regret for one more lost chance of understanding. If there was any message in Mrs. Perry's answering smile, Barbara couldn't read it.

Well, but I won't think about it, she said to herself, dressing hurriedly. I won't think about tonight either, she decided, and began to wonder what it would be like. I have never been to a party before. She felt a wrench of self-pity. To birthday parties, Fortnightlies, church parties. Never been to or given a party of selected people—the right age, the right people. There were other cliques in the school, but no others that interested her as this one did. How had the miracle occurred? Through Mrs. Howard? The accident of her initial? They could have dropped and forgotten her immediately, the night's caroling done. I must have done something, I must in some way have been nice, have seemed a person they'd want to know. Barbara Perry? Oh, but we must ask *her* to the party, really I had no idea what a lovely person she was until— Until what? Had it been her father's version of Hector that won them? No, something within herself. She had sung with them, sat in the kitchen, laughing and vivid—she could see herself now, hear her laugh—and they had realized that here was someone who would add to their group, who could share with them the secrets and the signals, the wild spirits and elusive melancholy, the purport of their age. I am about to become part of something, she said, and immediately had a vision of herself neglected, alone, wordless in a corner at Margaret Obemeyer's house, the party spinning around her like a kaleidoscope, an occasional pitying or puzzled glance tossed her way and withdrawn. *That dope in the corner? Barbara Perry. She always looks like she'd just buried someone in the cellar. Not even close to the most, Barbara Perry.* She sat down, hands pressed against her cheeks, knees tight together. Now, be calm. Calm down. It's only a party. You don't even have to go, if you don't want to. But you do want to. And the only reason you'd be wordless in a corner was . . . if you went in a corner and didn't talk. She smiled shakily.

You said you weren't going to think about it, didn't you? Last night you said you would think, and you didn't. Today you say you won't, and you do. Was it possible, was it even remotely conceivable, that you could discipline your own mind? It *was* your own, so why couldn't you make it behave? She remembered Katy saying once that there was a part of your brain, the oldest and most important part, that gave all the messages to the rest of you. "It's the part they give Miltowns to," Katy had explained. "Because if it starts giving too many messages, the rest of you goes all to pieces trying to keep up. I'm a wreck trying to keep up with mine, but of course I don't have any Miltowns."

"Mine's always telling me to forget it," Barbara had replied.

"Forget what?"

"Everything, I guess."

She thought now, severely and intently, of that part of her brain, letting her down, sending messages of defeat all over the place. "Just call me Miss Mess from Messville," said the oldest part of her brain. But the rest of her rose up in rebellion.

I am about to become part of something, about to begin my own life, so either you co-operate or keep out of it. She could almost *feel* a relaxation in her mind, a giving over of something that had wanted to keep her a child, afraid to leave a room clearly marked *Family*. There are rooms and rooms and rooms beyond this, she thought. And no reason why you should not return, but you have to know that there are others, have to venture and find them, and not be afraid. Profoundly stirred, feeling almost a martyr to her own resolution, she rose and went out to help her brothers build a snowman.

PART THREE

CHAPTER ONE

*Andrew and Richard, who were children still, com-*fortably walled in the Family room, could not notice any change in her, could have no way of knowing that suddenly she was free to walk through the door and back again, through a further door and back again, that she had begun a journey which would not end until she walked through the last door, which was Death and so distant that it need not be thought of (though it was strange that long ago, when she was where her brothers now unconsciously played, that last door had seemed at times so close and threateningly agape that she'd cried out in the night for her father, who had always come. She wondered whether Andrew and Richard, who never had nightmares, saw in some other, silent way, the door open, and the people they loved walk through, and the door close. She shivered briefly, remembering, and then forgot).

"The snow's awfully crumbly," she said, gathering a handful that powdered in her mitten.

Her brothers looked at her reproachfully, as though she'd drawn attention to a flaw in the character of Old Mother Nature. Together they turned away and began sweeping the snow, with their arms, into something approximating a mound. They patted and pawed, shored it up into a hill that collapsed, collected more snow and began again. Barbara suggested that they pour water over the hill, and went to the kitchen to fill a large pot, but it merely flattened what they'd collected, making an area of seepy gray, so they had to move to another part of the yard, and, in their usual fashion, were too preoccupied to notice whether she came along.

Because there was nothing else to do, Barbara trailed after them, now making no attempt to assist. "Why did you ask me at all?" she said to Andrew after a while.

"I thought you might like to help," he said, and added politely, "We like to have you."

Barbara smiled. "That's nice. The snow seems better here, anyway." Probably because they were now in a shady part of the yard. It was cold, but Andrew and Richard worked happily, their cheeks like pippins, noses running unattended.

"Let's make a snow rabbit," Richard said.

Andrew looked tempted. "We couldn't make his ears," he said doubtfully.

"You could make them droop," Barbara said. "And we could get straws out of the broom for whiskers." She was rewarded with a combined glance of rapture.

"Barby, that's *marvelous*," Andrew said, and she felt quite foolishly pleased, watching them work up a rather shapeless piece of sculpture which, with their joint effort, would presently be a rabbit. Or anyway, called one, Barbara thought. She kneeled at the back of the mound and tried to fashion a rabbit-like tail.

It was thus that Randy Lawson, driving by, saw her, and the picture seemed so charming to him that he stopped and rolled down his window, though he'd driven by this house time and time again, never even remembering that Barbara Perry lived here.

"Snowman?" he called.

"Snow rabbit," said Barbara, confused, shy, shaken with happiness, blessing Andrew with all her being for having invited her, however casually, into the yard. Randy would have driven past. He's probably driven past a hundred times, and he would have today, except that Andrew happened to ask me to help, and I happened to accept. What if I hadn't? she wondered, attacked with unnecessary regret. What if I'd done what I'd practically always do—gone up to my room to lie on the bed and dream about marvels that would happen *sometime*? What if—

"Snow rabbit?" said Randy, rubbing a hand over his blond crew cut. "Never heard of one."

"You just did," Andrew said factually.

Randy laughed, shifted gears, hesitated. "Could I help?" he asked, and sounded rather surprised at himself.

"No, thanks," said Richard.

But Barbara, from what depth of wisdom even she could not tell, merely smiled, and Randy got out of his car. Loose-limbed, graceful, sure of himself, he came through the gate and addressed himself to Richard. "Okay if I watch?" he asked.

Richard nodded. "It isn't easy," he explained.

"I can see it wouldn't be. What are you going to do about the ears?"

At such an intelligent question, Andrew and Richard capitulated, and the four of them set to work as though they'd spent their lives together in the snow, building rabbits.

"Say," Randy said suddenly, "where's your uncle?"

"Down the road, a lady's mile, trying to get back," Barbara murmured. She was, once again, quoting her father, but there was no need for Randy to know that. And he did seem quite taken with the words. His eyes rested on her face appreciatively. Taken by more than the words, Barbara thought dizzily, Oh, I can't support such happiness, such bliss—

"Uncle?" said Richard. "What uncle?"

"He means Hector," Barbara said.

"Hector?" Richard repeated.

Andrew, however, began to giggle. "Uncle Hector." He looked at Randy. "He's got a spell on him, you know. He's a police dog, ever since he lost the argument with the witch over—over—"

"Transformation," Barbara said.

"Yeah. Transformation."

"What does he look like when he's himself?" Randy asked.

"Well," said Andrew with mock seriousness, "we've never actually seen him himself, but Daddy says he's a big shaggy fellow. Isn't that right, Barbara?"

Barbara nodded. Uncle Hector is a big shaggy fellow, but I am a girl that Randy Lawson likes to look at. . . . *Andrew, Richard, I will never be cross with you again in my life.*

"He's a detective, no doubt," said Randy. The two boys doubled over with glee, and Hector took that moment to charge around a corner of the house, straight at them.

Mr. Perry, looking out of the sewing-room window, saw his three children, a blond boy and Hector in a farrago of laughter and barking. Something about the group struck him as so sunny and sparkling that he leaned forward, elbows on the window sill, and watched, as he would a play, the gradual subsidence of the laughter, the return to the snowman (a queerer looking snowman he had never seen). He wondered who the blond boy was. Handsome fellow, and definitely attentive to Barbara— He turned back to his work, feeling oddly lighthearted.

When his wife came upstairs to put linens in the closet, he called out, "How about some coffee, Mrs. Carlyle?"

"Did I hear you correctly?" she asked, coming to stand in the doorway.

"Coffee?"

"Carlyle."

He laughed. "Oh, well, who knows? Maybe next year I'll do an eighth-grade text, and then a twelfth-grade text, and the first thing we know I might be writing for real grown-up people. Like you."

She gave him a little grin that tilted her eyes. "Come and get your coffee, Thomas. Did you know that Barbara's going to a party tonight?"

"For Barbara," said Mr. Perry, with another glance out the window, "the party has already begun."

His wife walked over to see. "That's Randy Lawson," she said.

"Ah."

"What do you mean, ah?"

"Ah, who's Randy Lawson?"

"His father's a lawyer here in town."

"Oh, sure, George Lawson. He's on the school board. Looks dyspeptic. Has an excellent appreciation of other people's failings."

"That's the one."

"Carlyle refers to a man with good digestion as a peptician. Too bad we can't use words like that any more."

"Why don't you?" she asked. "Use it anyway."

"It wouldn't be understood. *Watch the great words go down.* Somebody or other said that. Besides me, that is."

"I don't think peptician is such a great word."

"You're carping. How about that coffee?"

He spoke with great geniality, and Mrs. Perry, going down to see about his coffee, thought she knew the reason why. Because Barbara was laughing in the company of a nice boy, because Hal worried (never saying anything) that she might not be popular, might not be liked, might not be happy. And now that he was presented with a picture that would erase some of his fears, he could afford to joke about Carlyle, and about himself.

In theory, Hal tended to be scornful of what he called "reference groups," those of your peers to whom you turned at all times, adjusting and fitting your ambitions, your ideology, your personality, to the group standard.

"This fear," he'd say, "of non-conforming is getting worse every year. From kindergarten on, we're driven into a mold. The child we value is the harmonious, reconcilable one, and if he isn't reconcilable, we cut and prune and pad until he at least *appears* to be, and the devil take his natural instincts. What a world of listlessness this harmony foretells."

She said to him now, as they settled in the living room, "It's nice for Barbara to be asked out by this particular group." He said nothing, so she added, "This particular reference group."

Hal held his pipe by the bowl, aimed the stem at her. It was a gesture she found excruciatingly annoying, though she had never said so. Long ago, Letty Perry had decided that the best of men—and Hal could surely be counted among the best of men—would have mannerisms calculated to drive a wife mad, if she permitted them to, and that the only solution was to accept them, as, so clearly, mannerisms of your own were accepted in silence. Still, she thought, her eyes on the pipestem, I always feel as if I were being held up.

"Don't think," he said, "that the snideness of your remark has escaped me. I have no defense. Yes, I have this defense—Barbara is caught by the system. She *wants* to be accepted by this group, to accommodate herself to its pattern. It is impossible for Barbara to live happily while she's unassimilated, and I happen to feel that happiness is healthy and necessary to the human being. What in the world good would it do Barbara to stand alone, to be unique, if it were only the result of rejection? What I deplore is the fact that people are becoming, more and more, herd creatures. I certainly don't want my daughter to be a maverick *yearning* for the brand. If it had been by choice . . . Andrew, I imagine, will never be part of a herd, but it'll be because he doesn't choose to be."

He put his pipe between his teeth, grumbled around it, "However, I refuse to become exercised about this matter. Young people have to make their way, take their chances. We do what we can for them, but the major portion of the job is up to them, just as it was up to us." He put the pipe in its rack, looked at his wife thoughtfully. "I don't suppose it would do a particle of good to point out to her that she's never going to be happy, or accepted by any group at all, until she stops thinking exclusively and constantly of herself?"

"You have pointed it out."

"Not in so many words."

"In practically those identical words," she said remorselessly.

He shifted in his chair, not answering, drank his coffee, said he supposed he might as well get back to work.

"All right—" she nearly said Mr. Carlyle, substituted dear. "I wouldn't worry about Barbara. She'll be all right."

"Sure, sure." He hesitated at the foot of the stairway. "Why don't you have her bring that boy in? Give him some cocoa, or something."

Letty looked at her husband with tenderness. "I'll wait. See what she decides."

"Yes, that's probably best." Still he didn't go. "Does it ever occur to you that it's too hard to be a parent?"

"But too late not to be."

"There's that," he said, and mounted the stairs.

CHAPTER TWO

*Richard had gotten straws from the broom for whisk-*ers, two prunes for eyes and a radish for a nose. Thus outfitted, the snow rabbit was startlingly successful, and the four of them paced around it, eying it from all angles.

"A very superior rabbit," Randy said, "no matter how you look at it."

Andrew and Richard nodded with the critical agreement of co-creators, Barbara with the absolute compliance of one who has just fallen in love. For there could be no question of it, she had fallen in love with Randy, and it seemed incredible that only yesterday she had said to herself Randy, or Max, or Jeff, as if he were just one of a group. But no—even as she thought, she convinced herself that she had selected him especially to think about. She really had—on the night of the caroling. It had been Randy she'd most noticed, Randy who'd been the radiant center of the assembly in the kitchen, Randy she'd thought of the next day. If she'd thought of Jeff and Max, too . . . well, it was only because they'd been there. You couldn't just block people from your mind, she said, not realizing that this was precisely what she did most of the time. And long before the caroling, she had noticed Randy in school, registered his height, and the light walk, and the quick, carefree smile. She hadn't —hadn't *coveted* him, because he'd seemed so far out of her reach that she might as easily have coveted—a star, she thought, reduced to triteness in the urgency of gathering this entire emotion quickly to herself.

And now here he was (Andrew, Richard, *thank you*) bestowing on her the beautiful smile, not seeming hurried, laughing with the boys, tousling Hector's head, again and again glancing over to meet her eyes. She could feel herself quicken to life at those glances. Feel, somehow, that she was shining with life, that her lashes were longer, her voice silken, her gestures endowed with grace. I shall always remember today, she thought. Always. What was that line her father quoted every now and then? *I've been born, and once is enough.* Well, once is not enough for me. I've been born, and now today I'm born again, and I'm in love, and why didn't I know that this would happen? That everything in my life was leading me to this moment, this aliveness, this love? She could feel her pulse like some fresh brook bounding secretly, dashingly toward the ultimate embrace.

Then Randy shot his wrist forward, looked at his watch. "Getting on," he said.

Oh, no! No, no, you *can't*. "I expect I could rustle up a cup of chocolate for you. That is, if you have time." Was that her voice, sounding so calm, covering the tumult of her discovery so efficiently?

He debated. "Sure, I have time. That'd be fine."

This is Randy Lawson beside me, and he's coming into my house with me, and we will sit together and have chocolate, and find words to say, and we will be together. Oh, pray that the boys want to stay out here, that Mother and Dad are busy, or will have the perception to become busy.

As they came in the kitchen, she heard her mother's voice on the phone. ". . . never seem to be able to make a sweet potato do anything but rot in the water. . . . You, too? Oh, well, avocados . . . every woman in America has to go through the avocado struggle at some point in her life. . . . Somebody told me you can grow a tree from lemon seeds, but somehow I never remember about it when I'm squeezing lemons—"

Oh, *Mother,* Barbara thought hopelessly, did you have to be having this conversation now? She said, lifting her voice, "Let me have your jacket. I'll put it in the closet."

"Don't bother," Randy said. "It'll be okay here." He

hung it over the back of a chair, and Barbara drooped a little. Putting the jacket away would have made his stay—however short—seem more permanent. But she couldn't insist.

"Well, I have to go now," Mrs. Perry was saying. "But do let me know how you make out with the azalea bush. . . . Yes, of course . . . 'By." She came into the kitchen, smiling, looking quite pretty, Barbara thought. But this eternal discussion of pits and plants—

"Mother, this is Randy Lawson," she said. "He sort of got to helping us with the snow rabbit."

"Snow rabbit?" Mrs. Perry said. "Oh, I must go and see. How are you, Randy?"

"Great, Mrs. Perry." He put out a large hand, shook hers vigorously.

"And your parents?"

"Okay," he said briefly. "Say, you ought to get together with my Aunt Constance. She's got these avocado pits all over the place. To tell you the truth, they look like a lot of little bald heads in jars to me."

"That was your aunt I was just talking to," Mrs. Perry said. She caught Barbara's blank expression, and explained, "Mrs. Frost."

"She's your aunt?" Barbara said to Randy. "I didn't know that."

Randy seemed to find that unanswerable. He smiled, nodded, then said to Mrs. Perry, "Say, did she ever tell you about the time she bought the fifty-year-old cactus from the dry cleaner? Well, it was in his window, and she's just bats over cactuses—cacti?—"

"Search me," Letty Perry said, and Barbara frowned slightly.

"She's bats about more than one cactus," Randy said. "So she was after this fellow for ages to sell it, and it took some persuading. She said he behaved as if she were trying to buy his child, but he gave in. Uncle George says she could have bought a piece of New Mexico for what she paid, but it was this particular cactus she wanted."

"And how is it?" Mrs. Perry said solicitously.

Randy shook his head. "Died in a week. We never could figure it out, except that maybe the poor thing was used to the fumes or something. I said, 'For Pete's sakes, Aunt Constance—' she was carrying on so '—now you're acting like the thing *had* been a child.' But she wouldn't answer me."

"Indoor gardening is a heart-rending pursuit," Mrs. Perry said. "You just can't know, until you've been bitten— Why, I spent a whole winter trying to nurse a nasturtium back to sanity, and almost lost mine doing it."

"What was wrong with it?" he asked gently.

"Disturbed. Oh, a very disturbed young plant."

Barbara listened to this exchange with confusion and dismay. He was being—he was being just as friendly and interested with her mother, in precisely the same way, as he had been with her. So that's all it amounted to, she thought bitterly. *Friendliness.* Swept from one extreme of emotion to another, with no time at all to adjust en route, she felt frozen with despair. Friendliness wasn't what she wanted from Randy. She wanted . . . Oh, but she wouldn't say what it was she wanted.

Abandoning hope, she said in a flat voice, "I was going to give Randy some cocoa."

Mrs. Perry glanced sharply at her daughter, bit back a comment. "Cocoa's a *splendid* idea, on such a day. Why don't you take it down in the cellar—in the rumpus room? I was just about to vacuum up here, so you wouldn't want to sit in the middle of that." Clear as a telegraph message, her voice said, *Barbara, you're behaving badly, pull yourself together*. "I think I'll go out and see what the boys have wrought."

It seemed she could never do anything right, it seemed that her strength was strewn like wreckage the length and breadth of her life, but Barbara made an attempt to assemble it. "We all wrought it," she said. The tone of her voice seemed to have picked up. "That rabbit was wrought by four of us, not just the boys." That was better. At least, her mother's nod seemed to say so. Randy, apparently, had noticed nothing out of the way. Why, for that matter, should he? He hadn't invested all his emotional capital in one hour this morning, and so had nothing threatened.

Entwined in the tentacles of so much feeling, aware of a glimmering but shaming recognition that it really was *too* much feeling, Barbara opened the refrigerator and wished she could crawl in for a moment, till the hotness in her cheeks and neck subsided. She clutched a quart of milk in unsteady hands and thought, If this is love, I don't think I'll ever really take to it, and then Randy was saying, "Oh, good, we're going to have plump cocoa."

In the need to find out what that meant, Barbara more or less forgot herself. "Plump cocoa?" she echoed.

Randy leaned against the sink, his eyes reminiscent. "It's . . . sort of a family saying—" He stopped short, and the silence lengthened till she rather thought he'd changed his mind about explaining it. He continued, abstractedly. "When I was a kid—we lived in Michigan, you know—" Barbara had not known, but nodded "—I asked the minister's sons in this small town we lived in to have some cocoa with me one day. That's how the saying arose, because when my mother made it with milk, one of the boys said, '*My* mother always makes *skinny* cocoa.' With water, you know," he explained. "I've always remembered it. Sort of sad."

Sharing this sadness, this recollection with him, Barbara began to be at peace again. What it is, she told herself, collecting china and silver on a tray in hands now more reliable, what it comes to is that I mustn't be so . . . so headlong. For a moment she forgot about Randy and took an almost detached look at herself. She had a lot of living left to do, a lot of mistakes to correct (and, inevitably, more to make), a lot of chances to take and decisions to make . . . she had an entire life ahead of her. The life that lay behind had been both lovely and badly mishandled (not only by her parents, she admitted, though she'd been inclined, till today, to apportion them the blame for whatever went wrong, and to credit the triumphs, when they came, to herself). But what was important in all this was that that life *was* behind. Today everything is different, is fresh. Today is a beginning.

Back in a flood came courage and highhanded hope, but now she recognized it with something like consternation. If I keep on like this, I won't live to be twenty. I'll be extinguished by sensation in a year. She saw herself reeling into an early grave, shredded feelings fluttering all around her, draperies of ecstasy and despair rended by her own lack of prudence.

"You aren't supposed to let the milk boil," Randy said, turning the gas off beneath the saucepan.

Barbara started. "Oh, my goodness. I'm sorry."

"No harm done. I caught it in time. Here, I'll carry the tray. You lead the way to the cellar."

"Rumpus room," she said automatically.

"In my house," he said, "it's supposed to be a rathskellar. But somehow it insists on its right to be a cellar, period."

He picked up the tray, and, on the way to the rumpus-room door, glanced into the living room. "That your father?" he asked in an aside. "Wouldn't want to go by without a word, or anything."

Barbara glanced morosely into the living room. She hadn't heard him come downstairs, but sure enough there sat Dad in his armchair, and not even reading, so that you could reasonably assume he was busy and not to be disturbed. Just sitting there, his forehead wrinkled, his eyes on space. He looked up when he heard them, got to his feet.

Well, there was nothing for it but to go in. She led the way. "Dad, this is Randy Lawson."

Randy inclined his head, looked at the tray he was carrying, set it down on a table—resting on some magazines so that the cups, saucers, pot and silver slid a little—and put out his hand. "Pleased to meet you, sir. How are you?"

"Fine, fine," said Mr. Perry. "Having cocoa?" He seemed to realize that this sounded inclusive, added hastily, "Never drink it myself."

But Barbara was beyond trying to get Randy in the rumpus room alone, and Randy quite obviously was prepared to have his cocoa anywhere. Or nowhere. Randy, she was beginning to think, found his nourishment in talking. It seemed in no way to lessen his quality, detract from his charm. Her own father held that conversation was man's greatest gift. "Not just the gift of speech, mind you," he'd say, "the art of conversation." Randy hadn't said anything particularly deep, but there was something appealing in his enjoyment of talk. There was, strangely, something reassuring, warming, in the fact that he talked so readily and comfortably with her parents.

He sat now, cocoa beside him, discussing books with her father (it appeared that Randy liked to read), and Barbara thought, I was the one who was wrong. Impolite, clumsy. . . . She wondered feverishly if he'd seen how she had tried to dispense with her family, so as to be alone with him. Disloyal. Oh, he must have noticed. Probably he'd almost perished with relief to see her father here, and so be spared the prospect of a quarter of an hour or more alone in the rumpus room with her. What did he think I wanted to do with him, anyway? Neck? Make a declaration of my feelings? She blinked back a tear, her stomach tight with humiliation. I should have said, Come and have some cocoa with my mother and father. I should have called the boys. And Hector. And maybe the turtle and the guppies could have been persuaded to attend. I should have said, Do come in, but heavens don't expect to be trapped with me alone for a *second*. . . .

Too late, too late.

Now, of course, he'll go away thinking what an elegant family I have, and what a pathetic, transparent creature I am. . . . Oh, I wish I were dead, she thought, forgetting that she'd just begun to live.

"Yeah, but some of these writers," Randy was saying, "are . . . you can *get* them. You know what I mean?

Hardy, now. The guy's the greatest, and you can *read* him. You get what he's saying. But this Kafka—" Randy lifted his shoulders, spread his big hands "—I read the thing—*The Castle*—and then I read it again, and I kept saying to myself, This is English, it's all words I can understand, but, boy, put them all together, they spell *nothing.*"

Mr. Perry smiled. "I have a theory about that. Some writers—not necessarily the greatest writers, but it applies to many of them, too—require the reader to read as creatively as the writer wrote." Randy sat forward, elbows on his knees, and Mr. Perry continued happily, "Now, take a man like Hardy. You can read Hardy almost passively, because he does all the work for you. It's wonderful, perceptive stuff, but he only demands your interest. But a man like Kafka, who seems confusing, or a man like Dostoevski, who *seems* straightforward, demands that you work with him, that you develop and create and strive in the reading almost as hard as he did in the writing. See what I mean?"

"Yes," said Randy thoughtfully. "Yes, I do. That's really interesting, the way you put it."

"It's been put better," Mr. Perry said, "but the kernel is there. Better drink your cocoa, it'll be cold." He looked quizzically at Barbara, made a tentative move to leave, but Randy was already addressing him again.

"This is a nice room," Randy said. "Sort of worn. Oh, sorry—"

Barbara burst into slightly tremulous laughter, as Mr. Perry hastened to assure Randy that no offense had been taken, and they all three looked soberly around the room that seemed to Barbara so napless, so thin, so dun.

"It's got that lived-in look," she said, her voice quite expressionless.

"Yeah, that's sort of what I meant," Randy said. There was a current of asperity between them that Barbara found rather revivifying. If he was going to walk out praising her family and her lived-in (lived-out) living room, and never bothering to call on her again (or, at least, not for herself—he might come back to discuss creative reading with her father), he wouldn't carry away a picture of her sitting in dumb misery on the sofa, a thing without spirit brooding over the frustration of not having him to herself. She sat, a stiff smile askew on her lips, showing him her indifference.

The back door burst open and the boys came hurtling in. "Mother's over at Ellen Murray's," Andrew explained, getting out of his jacket as if it were only to be subdued by force, and getting the snow off his boots by jabbing them at the hall rug. He looked at Barbara. "She said not to disturb you and Randy."

"We're planning to have a hole in the floor over there," Barbara said, waving her hand. "To grow a lemon tree in." Or hide in. Her face was flaming. Oh, to be able to bury it in her arms, or throw it away— But Randy and her father grinned at what she'd said, and she felt grateful to them, though they wouldn't know the reason why. People like Randy and her father didn't stumble into self-devised rejections and then have to wait helplessly for someone to give them a hand out. They knew where they were walking, people like that, even if not where they were going. It didn't seem to Barbara that anyone could really be sure where he was going. But they, at least, didn't careen awkwardly about, taking now a stab in that direction, now a stab in this, always winding up either up against a wall or trapped in a maze.

She remembered trying to explain to her father once how it always surprised her when someone who had offered to meet her, to call for her, actually did.

"How do you mean?" he'd asked gently.

"Oh, well . . . I mean, that if I'm supposed to meet somebody downtown, or if somebody says they'll come by for me in the car . . . I'm always sort of surprised if they do. Isn't that what I said?" she added. She hadn't told him how panicky she got, but somehow she couldn't. It sounded so *sick,* so wrong, even to herself.

Her father had agreed in a rather sad voice that that was what she had said. "It took me by surprise. Do you know why you feel this way?"

Shaking her head, Barbara had said she supposed she just thought they'd forget her. "Don't you ever feel that?" she'd asked.

"No. Never. I assume that people will show up, or call for me, if that was how it was planned."

"What if they didn't?"

"I'd assume something had gone wrong, Barbara. I wouldn't think they'd forgotten me." He'd gone on to say something else, but Barbara, sitting and thinking about all the fears and worries she had to cope with, didn't listen.

She thought of it now, though, and realized that that was the last time she'd attempted to have a talk—a close, personal talk—with her father. Nearly two years ago. It wasn't his fault. It wasn't, really, her own. But suddenly she recalled, as though she had never actually listened to them until this minute, in her mind, all his tentative, courteous offers of help. All of them spurned, turned aside as though she did not understand. She realized how many times, at some loose, ill-considered word or gesture of hers, her mother would lift her head and poise on the very brink of speech and then shy off, almost as if she'd been warned. *Do* I warn them? Barbara wondered. Have I warned them off often enough, nailed up enough signs saying *No Trespassing,* so that I am, finally, to be left in the middle of my isolation, my *exile* . . . unvisited, uninvited, unknown?

"Barbara, you're staring again," Andrew said nervously. "Make your eyes *look.*"

She blinked. "Look at what?"

"I don't care. Just don't make them like glass that way. I told you this before."

"We all do that from time to time," Mr. Perry said

mildly. "What's your mother doing over at the Murrays'?"

"Ellen's engaged man gave her a ring," Richard said. It sounded wonderfully formal, and Barbara caught Randy's amused eye on her brother. She wouldn't spoil it by telling him of the struggle with fiancé that finally resulted in this, far nicer, term. "Ellen said it's about time, and you'd need a telescope to see it, but come on over and look."

"Ellen said that?" Mr. Perry asked in horror.

Richard nodded, and Andrew said, "She yelled it across the street, and she said she was thinking of going to a business school instead. So Mother went over to look at the ring. Do they have a telescope?"

"Oh, ye gods," Mr. Perry muttered. "The things that get said. The things that people allow themselves to say."

"It's pretty rough," Randy agreed.

"A few weeks ago she was so mad about him she couldn't be bothered waiting till graduation," Barbara said. "But they talked her out of that. I mean, they talked her into waiting."

"It's disgusting," Mr. Perry said to no one in particular. "It's not tragedy—because the thing's usually on too low a level—but it's a pitiful farce that love is so easily confused with an inability to stay alone, or with a desire to get away, or with any one of a number of things which have no relation whatsoever to the really beautiful achievement of love."

Slightly stunned, Barbara looked at Randy to see how he was taking this, and found him mesmerized. Before today, she thought, I'd have died to have my father talk in such a way before someone my age. I'd never even have taken the time to find out how they felt about it, I'd have been so curdled with embarrassment. Yet there was Randy, accepting every word her father said, and obviously waiting for more. Was it just with somebody else's father you could feel like this? Was Randy this interested in his own father's disquisitions? No, he and his father had said practically nothing to each other that night in the car, and Randy hadn't sounded the least bit relaxed. If I talked to Mr. Lawson, and he to me, would this sense of recognition, of closeness, arise? She was pretty sure it would not. What do you mean, pretty sure? she asked herself. You know quite well that this is something Dad does to people. He has some quality that people respond to. You should be grateful to have such a man around you. Well, I am grateful. And for my mother and my brothers, too. They're extraordinary people, and I'm grateful. She thought this out and emerged feeling as resentful as she'd ever felt in her life.

And this on the day when she'd decided to grow up.

Oh, it was hopeless. She wished Randy, who was now discussing guppies with Richard, would go home. She wished he'd never stopped in the first place, had never left Michigan, never been born.

But he didn't leave for over an hour, during which time he covered the whole house, like a cat familiarizing itself with a place where it means to stay. He talked with the boys, he talked with her father. Her mother came back, and he talked with her.

"In fact," she burst out, when he had finally gone, "he talked to everybody in the place including the turtle. Except *me*." She was alone with her father and mother in the living room, and so angry that all the coolness and reserve developed over the past three years had fallen from her beyond any hope of present recapture.

"Perhaps because you didn't talk to him?" her father suggested, busy with his pipe and not looking up.

"He doesn't get much conversation at home," Mrs. Perry pointed out. "An only child, in a home where the parents almost don't talk to each other. Just having a chance to talk—"

"He has plenty of chances to talk in school, and plenty of friends," Barbara snapped.

"Oh. Possibly I meant . . . talk with a family. Something like that," Mrs. Perry said, experimentally, cautiously.

"Does everybody have to be so *understanding?"* Barbara yelled. She could hear herself yelling, and had no way at all to stop. She'd taken her finger from the dike for a moment, and now everything crumbled and the waves came at her. "Listen to me, both of you . . . I'm *growing up!* Do you understand that? You're so good at understanding, try it out on that. I've been invited to a party with people that matter, even if Dad does call them a clique, and I've done a whole lot of thinking today, and I am not a child any more! *See?*" She stopped, panting, ashamed, furious. "Well, *say something!*"

"Shut up," said Mr. Perry.

CHAPTER THREE

After Barbara had gone running upstairs, her parents sat looking at each other speculatively for a few moments.

"A bit rude, weren't you?" Mrs. Perry said at length.

"As a matter of fact, I think I was rather restrained." He lifted his eyebrows, blew out a long breath. "A bit rude, maybe. But I couldn't think of anything else to say. Another minute and she'd have been hysterical. She'd have said something that would have made her so ashamed she wouldn't have been able to speak to us for weeks. As it is, she'll probably have difficulty."

"It might have been better to let her have it all out now."

"If I was wrong, I'm sorry. I don't think it's a kindness—I don't even think it's a good catharsis—to let people drop all restraint and say a lot of things they'll regret miserably later on. The girl is steering a precarious enough course without having to add the kind of embarrassment that comes from having had your say when you were angry." He picked up his pipe. "In my opinion—"

"If you point that thing at me," Mrs. Perry interrupted, "I'll shoot it out of your hand."

"What?"

"I said I'm tired of having you underscore your points by leveling that thing at me as if it were a revolver."

"Well, I'll be . . ." He returned the pipe to its rack, scratched his head.

Silence fell, lengthened. They both began to speak at once, subsided, started up again, laughed nervously.

"You first," he managed to get in.

"No. No, I really don't know what I wanted to say. Something about Barbara, I suppose. Or something about life. She says she's growing up. Why did she tell us, do you suppose? I mean, why did she pick today to tell us?"

He shook his head. "I don't know. Something to do with that young fellow, maybe. Or the party she's been invited to. I wish I'd never used the word clique, but then I wish I'd never done and said a lot of things, plenty of them I don't even recognize, probably. But then, if it hadn't been those, it would have been others. Implementing our human right to err—"

He went on, but Mrs. Perry interrupted again. "Why today?"

"Probably it's like a boil coming to a head—" he began.

"Do you have to use such *revolting* expressions?" she flared.

Her husband looked at the ceiling. "Sorry," he mumbled. After another uneasy silence, "Well, the stone's been tossed in the pond and here come the ripples, and there's nothing to do about *that* except hope to ride them out."

"Hal, excuse me," she said.

"Life looks like becoming one long apology," he observed. The phone rang. "Let's not answer it."

Letty Perry walked over and picked up the receiver. "Hello. . . . Oh, Katy . . . how are you? Yes, I'll call her." She looked around (like someone noting the escape hatch, her husband thought), walked to the foot of the stairs and called, "Barbara . . . there's someone . . . I mean, Katy's on the phone for you."

A long pause, and then Barbara's voice. "Tell her I'll be there in a second." Another pause, followed by, "Thank you."

"When are they putting that extension in?" Hal asked.

"Monday."

"Monday. I suppose we can live till then." He got to his feet. "I think I'll go somewhere and whittle. Always thought I'd like to take up whittling, and there's no time like the present."

They were both making for other parts of the house when Barbara came down, red-eyed, but apparently calm. She held up a rather imperious hand. "Could you wait a second? I'd like to say something to you."

Without looking at each other, Mr. and Mrs. Perry settled in chairs to wait as they were told.

"Katy?" said Barbara. "I'm in a . . . Tonight? No, I'm sorry . . . I can't. No, it isn't that. . . . Well, if you insist, it's because Margaret invited me to a party, and . . . Well, that certainly isn't a very nice way to put it, but since you ask, I don't know how it *happened* that she . . . Okay, okay . . . sure, I'll see you tomorrow. . . . Yes, well, good-by."

She hung up, turned to face them, drew a deep breath and said, "I'm sorry for the way I acted."

Mr. Perry said, "I was just saying to your mother that we're apparently about to embark on what in later years will be referred to as our Abject Period." He caught his wife's severe expression, lifted his shoulders a little. "There's not much humor coming through today, is there?"

"Not for lack of trying," Mrs. Perry said.

"See what I've done," Barbara said. "I've even gotten you two mad at each other."

"Don't take all the credit," Mr. Perry said. "Your

mother and I can stir up a commendable scene between us without outside help."

Barbara said nothing. Mrs. Perry said aloud, but to herself, "Contrary. Just as contrary as he can be."

The phone rang.

Mr. Perry leaped to his feet. "That thing was put on earth to try men's souls. I'm going for a walk." He went out quickly. His wife, after a glance at Barbara, went upstairs to read. If I can, she thought. If my head will stop buzzing.

"Hello?" said Barbara. "Why, hello, Randy. . . ." Her voice softened, and then she thought, Probably he's forgotten something, left his muffler or—"What can I do for you?"

"Why . . . uh—" He sounded nonplused, and she realized her tone must have been sharper than she'd intended.

"Didn't mean to sound abrupt," she said. "I've been . . . having a tussle with my French homework. French always makes me belligerent." False, false. She liked French better than any other subject. Why sacrifice it? Does everybody find it this easy to lie, or is it just me?

Randy laughed. "You do homework over Christmas?"

"Oh, not really," she said hastily. "Just some I had to make up." Not a grind, don't let him think that.

"Thought for a minute we were kindred spirits," he said, and her heart simply dropped. Was there any way to recoup? "I find myself doing Latin declensions when there's absolutely no reason in the world for it," Randy was going on. "Or trying to read Virgil on my own. Peculiar."

But I try to read French books on my own, Barbara mourned, now unable to tell him, to share this peculiarity with him, without exposing herself as a liar. No, there was still a way—"I'm like that about *books,* too," she said, a little breathily. "It's just the grammar that gets me down." That wasn't true either. She had no trouble with grammar, but apparently something must be lost in the act of salvage. Something besides face, that was.

But now Randy made no further comment on the matter. Because he didn't believe her? Because he didn't care one way or another whether or not they were kindred spirits?

"How about it?" she heard him say.

How about what? she thought in despair. "I'm *sorry,* Randy," she said. "I didn't hear you. . . . The thing is, Hector got tangled up in the cord just as you spoke, and—" Was there to be no end to this? Starting tomorrow, she said to herself, no, starting the minute I hang up this phone, I'm going to tell *nothing* but—just in time she dropped that line of thought and managed to hear him ask if she'd like to have him stop by and pick her up on the way to the party.

Like it? she thought, swimming away on a tide of bliss. Does he have any idea of his power to give happiness? Does he realize—

"Well, how about it?" he said. "You're the most difficult person to talk to I've ever met in my life." The way he said it was not uncomplimentary, but on the other hand it didn't give her a sense of happy uniqueness. It was—

"Oh, sure, Randy. I'd love it," she said, decided she'd better qualify, and added, "That would be very nice."

After she'd hung up, she wondered how he'd known she was going to the party. Probably he'd talked to Margaret. Or to Connie Frost, his cousin. Funny, how I didn't know Connie and he were cousins, she thought, and paused. I didn't know that, nor that Katy wanted to be a doctor, nor that Mother knew Mrs. Obemeyer. I didn't recognize Mr. Irwin when he wasn't behind his counter. And I could go on with a similar list for hours, probably. A list of things I've never taken the trouble to find out, or register if I heard them, of people I've met and forgotten. And how many times have I done what I just did with Randy—lost the thread of a conversation completely because I'd wandered off in my own speculations?

"Woolgathering," her father had said once, not too long ago, "can doubtless be a mark of genius, but in my book it's more often a lack of consideration for other people, or interest in them."

She had scarcely listened. He'd been talking about someone at the college, hadn't he? One of his students, or a teacher. The remark probably would have passed out of her consciousness altogether, if he hadn't said woolgathering. Such an attractive word, which she had immediately taken unto herself, but not at all in the manner her father had been implying. *Woolgathering* . . . a meadowy, lazy, dream-headed word that couldn't help but make you feel different, special, someone whose present bore so little relation to her spangled future that she could scarcely be expected to take notice of people and incidents on this level. Barbara Perry? Yes, well I remember how absent-minded she seemed as a child, though of course we couldn't know then. . . . Yes, a *woolgathering* child, you know . . . always disappearing with a book to read all day in the branches of a gnarled old apple tree . . .

In strict fact, there wasn't any tree around here big enough to disappear into and read in all day. In stricter fact, she'd never really wanted to read in a tree, but it was something you would almost have to tell the reviewer from the *New York Times*. How could you be a world-famous writer if you hadn't sat all day in an apple tree reading books when you were a child? It would even do if you became an actress. You could have been reading Ibsen. It would do, as a matter of fact, for a childhood incident to fit any splendid future. . . .

But supposing, she thought now, just supposing you decided to look at it in another way. Supposing, further, that her father had not been talking about a student or a teacher at all, but to her, in his oblique fashion meant to be kind (Oh, well, she decided moodily, admit it *is* kind. Admit *something*. Okay, so I've admitted it), why then you emerged not as a young girl given to reverie and daydreaming, but as a person who just didn't care what anyone else looked like or was saying. *Sad and selfish,* Andrew had said, and whom had he been quoting?

I don't know. I don't know and I don't want to know, but this is *awful*.

She felt odd. A little dizzy, and sort of out of proportion, somehow. She moved, tottered, to the nearest chair, and sat down, running her tongue over dry lips. Is this what I am really like? False, indifferent, selfish and sad? But if that is so, then today is not a beginning. There can be no beginning. There can be no going back and repairing so much, so *much*. . . .

Her mother came in, looked at her, came to her side quickly, putting a light hand on her shoulder. "Barbara," she said with concern. "What's wrong?"

Barbara got up, looked in her mother's eyes. "I am facing myself," she said quietly. "And I don't like what I see."

Locked in each other's gaze they stood, Barbara's face a mask of wood, her mother's a study of conflict.

Finally Mrs. Perry said, "Don't you . . . don't young people ever give themselves another chance?"

"I don't know what you mean," Barbara said, but only to keep her mother talking. Which, she spared a moment to think, is certainly a change.

"What I'm trying to say is—you convict yourself all of a sudden of everything wrong. . . . I presume that's what you're doing?" Barbara nodded, wordless, and her mother went on, "But after the conviction, can't you give yourself another chance? To do better, to change? To . . . go on from there?"

"It's too late."

"Oh, *Barbara.* Barbara, for heaven's sake, this is *compounding* wrong. You're young, and full of lovely qualities—"

"I'm selfish, sad, inconsiderate—"

"Stop."

They both stopped and stared at each other. Then Mrs. Perry resumed slowly, "We all have periods of disliking ourselves. Most of us. And let me tell you, dear, the people who don't know such moments are the frightening and hopeless ones. They're convicted and they don't even know it, and they *never* have a second chance because they don't know they need one. But they suffer, and the people around them suffer." Her voice trailed off, picked up again. "Do you know, it isn't even really a matter of a *second* chance. I'm probably on my several hundredth, or maybe more. But I give myself these chances."

"Why?"

"Well," Letty Perry said simply, "probably because I like myself."

In spite of herself, Barbara stiffened.

"You think that sounds arrogant?" her mother asked.

"It isn't, actually. I'm a nice person. I have value. I wouldn't have the children I have, or the husband, if that weren't true. And what would happen to me, what would already have happened, if I'd succumbed to a period of . . . of self-contempt? What sort of a mother or wife or *person* would I be now?"

Barbara sniffled. This moment was stretching intolerably. What her mother was saying was right, was wise, but she wanted to go somewhere and sort it out. This day was stretching intolerably. Was it really still today? It seemed to have been going on forever, and there was still tonight to get through.

What am I saying? she thought. Tonight to *get* through? Tonight was the party, was Randy, was the beginning of life. Ah, so now you're willing to admit a beginning again? she asked herself, somewhat sourly. Can't you stick to anything? Then, immediately on the heels of that, Can't you give yourself another chance?

"Look," her mother said, "why don't you go to your room and lie down?"

Barbara stared in wonder. What a beautiful, sensible, simple suggestion. I never would have thought of it. She realized now that she was tired, all through her limbs, all through her bones and her mind and her heart. Exhausted by the complications of so much emotion. But she would never have thought to go and lie down.

"Thank you," she said to her mother. "It's a marvelous idea. Thank you . . . for everything." She turned and went upstairs. She thought—knew—that if she turned around she'd find her mother's eyes still on her, pensive, loving. But she didn't turn around.

She thought—knew—that when she lay down she would meditate on this strangest of days, would probe and burrow till she came to its heart, its significance. And then, she assured herself drowsily, everything will be clear to me. Everything in the world. Or, at least, everything in mine. . . .

But it was as if the day, which she had planned to hold and examine, as one would examine a puzzle, or a flower, became something that overflowed her hands and lapped around her whitely, like combers, and drowned her gently, and she slept.

CHAPTER FOUR

"Look," Mr. Perry said to Randy, who arrived ahead of time that evening, "why don't you give me a ring when you're ready to go home, and I'll pick you up? No reason why the boy's father should have to do all this taxiing all the time." He gave the impression (not meaning to, his wife knew. Hal was a man completely without guile) that Barbara was constantly being called for by boys and their fathers.

Before he could say anything to spoil it, Mrs. Perry said quickly, "That's a good idea, Randy. Why don't you tell your father?" Mr. Lawson had not come in, as Mr. Irwin had, but was waiting out in the car.

Randy hesitated. "Well, I'll ask him. It's very nice of you, sir. Tell you what, if I call, then you'll know Dad agreed, and if I don't call you'll know he's coming for us. Saay—" he said, his face lighting up as Barbara came in the room. "You look great."

Barbara looked like thousands of other young girls all over the country starting out on dates. That is to say, spirited, rosy, pretty and full of hope. The navy wool clung to her figure softly, flared over a crinoline, she had loops of gold beads at her throat, her bracelets clinked as she moved her arms, and her hair gleamed with something of gold in it too.

Her father, utterly spent by the day, looked at her with pleasure and surprise. Mrs. Perry was pleased, but she knew too well the resilience of women to be surprised at Barbara's appearance. A nap, some lipstick and the prospect of a party were sufficient to dispel signs of greater ravages than Barbara had suffered today . . . though Mrs. Perry did not underestimate how real the turmoil had been. But this was a quality women had (which often led to their being thought more wanting in sensibility than men), this of putting on a new dress, a new scent, and so facing down, temporarily, confusion and sorrow. But then, women by nature were more optimistic than men. I suppose, she thought, it comes from their ability to ignore facts when there is simply no point in facing them. Which, looked at narrowly, was fact-facing in the ultimate degree. She supposed Hal wouldn't agree with her, but he was an implacable fact-facer. He sometimes reminded her of those heroes in fairy tales who wrestled with a thing that kept changing shape in their arms—now a serpent, now a swan, now a flaming bush. A woman at some point would open her arms, drop the changeling and walk away. She wouldn't win half the kingdom, of course, but she'd keep her sanity and health. Maybe it's why women live longer than men, she mused. They know how to refuse a fight.

And so Barbara, who'd been going through a battle all day with herself, her life, her philosophy and her family, had now declared an amnesty, erased all signs of conflict from her person, and looked simply lovely. The thing to bear in mind, Mrs. Perry told herself, is that this kind of amnesty doesn't last. Let us give thanks for present good, but don't go trying to build a future on it.

When Barbara and Randy had gone, Mr. Perry sighed, sank deeper in his chair. "She's really very pretty," he said. "Will she have a good time at this party?"

"I think so. I . . . had a little talk with her this afternoon."

"Another one? It seems to me that life is made up of little talks with Barbara. I wish I could feel they helped."

"Perhaps this one did. She asked for it. That makes a difference."

"What are the boys doing?"

"Playing Monopoly. In the rumpus room."

He smiled. "Did I ever tell you that poem 'Growing Up'?"

Mrs. Perry shook her head.

"When I grow up I'll carry a stick
And be very dignified,
I'll have a watch that will really tick,
My house will be tall and built of brick,
And no one will guess that it's just a trick,
And I'm really myself inside."

"Oh, that's adorable," Mrs. Perry said. "Where did you find it?"

"I've forgotten. I've known it since I was a kid. Made sense to me then, and it makes sense to me now, in a different way, of course. *I'm really myself inside.*" He sighed, half-humorously. "Portrait of a successful human being. Are you really yourself inside, Letty?"

"Sometimes I think so. I'm not always sure."

"It's your doubts that assure your success. I'm glad she asked you for a talk."

"Let me tell you a poem *I've* known since I was a child. It made no sense then, and lots now," she said. "It's called 'Grown-up.' Edna Millay.

"Was it for this I uttered prayers,
And sobbed and cursed and kicked the stairs,
That now, domestic as a plate,
I should retire at half-past eight?"

Hal grinned. "Oh, the irony of it, the irony of it," he said, and then, "Well, I sure hope she has a good time at that party."

CHAPTER FIVE

Mr. Lawson didn't say, It took you long enough. But he might just as well have, Barbara thought. They scarcely had the door closed before he was driving down the street, and it wasn't until Randy said, "You remember Barbara Perry, Dad," that he spoke.

"Evening," said Mr. Lawson, not looking around.

"Good evening, Mr. Lawson," she said, and remembered to add, "It's nice of you to drive us."

No reply. Randy let out an almost inaudible sigh. "Mr. Perry said he'd pick us up, if you like." There was again the tension in his voice that Barbara had noticed on Christmas Eve.

"I ever say I minded picking you up?" Mr. Lawson asked.

"No, Dad. That wasn't it at all. He just said it . . . to

be helpful. He says there's no reason why the fathers of the boys should do all the taxiing."

"I never said I minded picking you up."

"No. No, of course not."

The matter was dropped there, and apparently settled, because when he let them out at Obemeyer's, Mr. Lawson said, "Call when you're ready," and drove off.

The second his father was gone, Randy seemed to forget his tension. Almost, Barbara thought, in the manner of a very young child, who releases the scolding adult from his mind the moment the actual presence is removed. Probably he'd had to develop this faculty, if his father was always as taciturn, as difficult to reach, as he'd seemed on the two occasions Barbara had met him. She thought this, and then, from her mind, too, Mr. Lawson was dispatched.

There was something more compelling, more urgent, that occupied not only her mind, but somehow her body—especially her chest, a cage against which her heart beat in anxious anticipation—and the something was PARTY, spelled in huge, wavering characters, like the lettering on billboards for mystery movies. She remembered the last time she'd been to a horror show, she'd asked her mother, who'd already seen it, what it was like. "Brr . . ." her mother had said. "It'll age you ten years. But then, you can afford it." The movie hadn't but she thought this party was likely to. Going up the flight of shallow brick stairs to the large brick house, she realized that she really was terrified. Impossible to go forward, impossible to retreat. Age me ten years, she thought, trying to wrench herself into a humorous frame of mind. Well, maybe it'd be a good thing. Age her a few, anyway. She could use aging.

Insensible of Randy's light hand on her elbow, her eyes blurred with apprehension, she still tried to say to herself, in a steadying firm way, that aging was a good process and tonight was a good time to embark upon it. Tonight, she instructed herself, I shall not *woolgather*. Just for tonight I'm going to live in the present, hear what people have to say. *Watch and join*. Put that on your escutcheon, and please don't blot. I'm going to care about the present, and if fancies have to be woven, they'll be woven when I am home and in bed. The very thought of being home and in bed, with the party, and the necessity to watch and join, behind her, filled her with so much yearning that she stopped and turned to Randy with a pleading look.

"Something wrong?" he asked.

"I . . ." *Why* was it so difficult to get a good deep breath? "No, nothing. I just . . . thought of something for a moment."

"You sure are a chip off the old professor," he said, and added at her uncomprehending look, "Is your father absent-minded, too?"

"Oh." She shook her head. "No. He's about the most present-minded person I know."

"Marvelous guy," Randy said feelingly, and then at the foot of the stairs another car drew up, discharging Jeff, Connie, Max and Alice. Immediately behind them (they'd been chauffeured by Mr. Maxwell) came Peter Adams, driving his own car, a souped-up convertible with an exhaust that could be heard in the next century and a horn that quacked like a duck. He was in their grade, had been old enough to drive for over a year and, in his own words, would never constitute a threat to the world's brainier citizens.

"Still, I've got a nice disposition," Barbara had heard him say once, "and my mother says it's a pleasure to cook for me. A guy can't have everything."

Sonia Bemis was beside him. Barbara found Sonia one of the most alarming people in school. Handsome, efficient, nearly always right (and undismayed when she was not), she had an imperious manner that brought out everything unassertive in Barbara, who resented her deeply, in silence, in the manner of unassertive people who see the imposition coming and can do nothing to ward it off. With Sonia, there had never been any possibility of rationalizing, of saying to yourself that after all you really loved to help, you were generous by nature. No, with Sonia the relationship was clear. She took advantage of anyone she could, you all but asked to be taken advantage of, you both pretended not to recognize the situation, both of you did, and, naturally, you disliked each other.

At least, Barbara thought with a rush of spirit and frankness, maybe she doesn't take time to dislike me, but I certainly don't care for her. Since in Barbara's philosophy it had always been necessary to find something to like in everybody (so being spared the humiliation of currying favor from those you did not admire) this was quite an exhilarating admission, on the tide of which she was able to sweep with the others into the house, toward the actuality of the party.

Having achieved this, the house itself then awed her back to timidity. Barbara was not accustomed to opulence, and though the Obemeyer house was not actually opulent, it was large and daringly decorated, and Barbara couldn't tell the difference. The center hall was high-ceilinged and wide. A staircase mounted to a landing and thence to the second floor. It was not a graceful staircase, but it was open and impressive and later, in describing it, she naturally used the word graceful. Hall and stairway were carpeted in scarlet broadloom, the walls papered in a lacy gray and white design. To the right, the double doors were closed; those on the left opened on a large living room, where a fire burned and a lovely old mirror above the mantel calmly reflected a lot of tremendous modern furniture, a great brass bowl filled with lemon leaves and white chrysanthemums, and heavy draperies drawn against the night. The colors were green, gray and yellow. The whole was rich, fresh, unfrayed. Barbara thought it was the most beautiful house she'd ever seen, and tried to take some comfort in the fact that nowhere could she see a book.

"Here, everybody," said Margaret, "come and put your things in the library."

She led the way down the hall, and Barbara, following with the others, realized that she was going to have to meet this house on its own terms. She hadn't really seen much of the Frosts' house except the kitchen, but it too had spoken of standards far beyond what the Perrys knew. Were all these people rich? Oh, well, she revised, knowing they were not in the real sense of the word wealthy, were they all so much better off than her family that she would have to abandon forever the notion of giving a party in the rumpus room at home? Ashamed of herself (but also ashamed of her rumpus room), she returned with the rest of them to the living room, feeling a goat among sheep, and wondering if she could baa convincingly enough to fool them.

Because I do want to fool them, she admitted to herself. I want to be accepted in the fold. *Barbara Perry? Oh, she's delicious. I mean, her father is this genius type who doesn't care a bit about material things, and they have this Alcotty home going all to pieces in a scholarly sort of way, all books and bats and cobwebs, you know—*

Barbara shook her head. My mind, she thought, is getting out of hand. If I'm going to go around making up answers to questions that will never be asked, at least I can make up *pleasing* answers. Or give up the habit altogether. She was not at all sure she could do that, but it was worth a try. For tonight, anyway, she reminded herself.

"This is a lovely room," she said to Margaret.

"Glad you like it—" Margaret began, and then, "Jeff! Come *back* in here. And stay *away* from the dining-room doors."

Jeff came across the hall. "I was only going to check, to be sure there weren't any crooks in the canapés."

"The Pinkerton men will take care of that," Margaret assured him.

Barbara, with a brightly amused expression, had a peculiar feeling of having gone through this scene before, but couldn't place it. She abandoned the effort, smiled, and happened to catch Randy's eye. He smiled warmly back. Wasn't I in love with him this morning? she thought. She wasn't in love with him now. She thought him fine and at least more familiar than anyone else here. She hoped he'd protect her until she became an accredited sheep (surely she could become one?) but she was far too busy trying to get the tone of the baa to spare any thought for love. Later, she thought, deciding to feel that she and Randy were fated for each other. Later on, I will fall in love with him again, and he will be the one who puts his arms around me and holds me, and says, Barbara, I love you . . . I am so much in love with you— His blue eyes and her hazel ones meet in a long exchange, and his arms tighten, and he puts his lips gently on hers. Barbara, I love you. . . .

"How are you, Barbara?" said Sonia Bemis. She looked tall, trim, cool as a flower. "Nice to see you. Did you have a good Christmas?" She dropped to a long couch. Cushions of down, Barbara noticed. It seemed almost sacrilege to destroy their puffiness, but she sat down beside Sonia as if commanded.

"Marvelous," she exclaimed. "I got the most marvelous camel hairs—I mean, camel's-hair coat." She bit her lip.

Sonia laughed. "I think camel hairs is cuter."

Barbara eyed her mistrustfully, with rising hope. Why so nice? Why . . . But then Max sat down with them, and with relief she shifted her regard to him. He was looking at Sonia, patting her long white fingers with his own rather stubby ones.

"Why don't you play the piano for us, girl?" he asked.

At one end of the room there was a rather square, blond mahogany baby grand piano. Barbara thought it was ugly, changed her mind when Sonia glanced over at it and said, "That elegant thing. Perhaps I will, a little later."

Max now looked at Barbara. "I play by ear," he told her.

"Oh, but that's marvelous." There *must* be another word for wonderful besides marvelous.

"Yup. Put my head down on the keyboard and wiggle my ear. It's sensational."

Barbara recoiled, her cheeks flushing darkly. She was being made fun of. The awful boy was making fun of her, right in front of everybody. She had a panicked sensation that upon this moment everything stood or fell. Somehow she could do the right thing, now, and be one of them, or she could shiver here in her humiliation and declare herself forever unacceptable. And there was only a moment, there was less than a moment, to decide her fate. Annihilation yawned at her feet, at the last second she stepped aside, contrived to laugh and said, "Do you play with both ears?"

It wasn't perfect. It wasn't, in Barbara's opinion, even close, but Max looked at her with some approval. "Just with the right," he said. "My left ear's tone deaf."

That struck Barbara as quite amusing, and this time her laugh was genuine.

" 'Pon my word," Sonia said languidly. "A straight man for you, Max."

Before Barbara had a chance to react one way or another to this, Max said in a pleased way, "I knew I'd have to get one someday, but I never knew it would come in such a pretty box."

Is this it? Barbara wondered breathlessly. Is this acceptance? Am I . . . oh, *am* I . . . beginning to look like a sheep? She couldn't help smiling at this, and Jeff Irwin, coming over to join them, looked at her closely, tipped his head and said, "She has private thoughts. She has private, pleasant thoughts, and she sits smiling at them."

"She's smiling at *me,* man," said Max. "I made a humorous sally, and she's still seeing the humor in it."

"That true?" said Jeff, pulling up a chair. "This fellow amuses you?"

Here she would have to move delicately. To say nothing would be dull. To say, Oh, he devastates me would be . . . too familiar. She wasn't that close to them yet. Not quite on *baaing* terms, she thought, and just prevented herself from giggling. No hysteria, now.

"He said something pretty funny," she admitted.

Jeff snapped his fingers. "And I not on hand to appreciate it. You wouldn't care to run through it again, Max, my boy? No? Well, that's a relief. Why are we hovering around up here? Why aren't we down in the game room?"

Game room, Barbara thought. Call it what you will, it's always in the cellar. She was rather relieved that they weren't going to remain all evening in this intimidating room. She thought this, and then wondered how a person could conquer the world if she became overpowered by a large living room in Nortown, Ohio. Good thing I don't have to start conquering it right away. Take care of tonight, she told herself, and the world will still be waiting. Just manage tonight.

"Search me," Max said in answer to Jeff. "But don't

take away my six-shooter. I may have to use it on Adams tonight. He's over there flirting with Alice."

"He isn't flirting," Sonia said calmly. "He's trying to see who he's talking to."

"Hey, yeah. I thought there was something different about him tonight. He break his cheaters?" said Jeff.

"Lost them, he says. I think he just feels prettier without them."

"If I ever lose my mind and ask you for a date," Max said, "will you promise to refuse?"

"It's a deal," said Sonia. Her composure was perfect. "Oh, by the way, in answer to your question, I believe we're waiting for Bud Parker to show."

"Parker's coming?" said Jeff.

"He took Margy to the movies last night, and she asked him to come. I think she likes him."

"Why not? He's a nice guy. Quiet, of course," Jeff said.

Sonia quirked an eyebrow. "Silences don't have the same effect on all of us that they have on you, Jeffy."

Jeff pulled his shoulders in. "My seconds will call on you in the morning. Not tomorrow morning. They're otherwise occupied. But any morning after that within the next ten years, you can expect them." He got to his feet. "And now, I'm leaving the field, before anyone gets hurt. Especially me. I'm so easily hurt." He glanced at Barbara. "You better come along, too. You don't look strong enough to cope with Sonia."

How right you are, Barbara thought. It might be a joke to Jeff, but to her Sonia represented a real threat. A casual thrust from that sharp tongue could topple the delicate framework of security she was building up. She paused uncertainly, saw that Sonia had transferred her entire attention to Max, got up and followed Jeff, who seemed to forget her as he joined Peter Adams. Barbara hovered a moment, not sharing their conversation, but attempting to seem part of it. It was best not to get detached from people and conversation long enough to seem forlorn, or uninterested. Either would be dangerous right now, though all right enough for those who belonged. Oh, the longing, the longing for what at times she affected to despise, for what, at times, she truly did despise. Snug, smug, safe little circles, revolving in their narrow orbits, unconscious of a world, of a universe, beyond. Parochial, provincial Pharisees. Women's clubs, fraternal organizations, high-school sodalities. The willingness, the eagerness, to associate with people who meant nothing to you. The sense of precarious triumph at having wrung a moderately friendly word from Sonia Bemis. What did she care about Sonia Bemis? And yet, she did, she did.

Her father, who had quite a few friends but very few acquaintances, held it a rule not to perpetuate relationships where there was no value on either side. "It is a waste of time (he could conceive no more grievous waste) and an abrasive to the spirit to drift into and prolong associations that have nothing more to justify them than propinquity, or mutual boredom. We pace this way but once, and I don't intend to clutter up my journey with expedient, or lazy, relationships."

Generally when he talked this way (as if the words were intended to be written rather than spoken) Barbara didn't listen. But this time she'd been interested. "You mean every acquaintance should be *productive?*" In her own mind, this was a charge of opportunism.

But, "Yes, that's just what I mean," he'd answered. "Productive, meaningful, on both sides, or in my book it's just no go. And let me tell you something else. In these . . . expedient associations . . . the thing cuts both ways. People ask you for dinner because you've asked them. You go because it would be rude not to, and you ask them back because it would be rude not to, and on and on. Ennui come full circle. What it comes to is—no matter how you doll it up—you go because you're afraid that if you don't the people won't like you, will say something about you. What if they don't like you? What if they do say something about you? This is one life we have. Are we going to spend the greater part of it trying to make everybody like us, and say nice things behind our backs? A pox on that."

"And yet," Barbara said, feeling that now she really had him, "Mother is friendly with everybody, with absolutely everybody."

"Your mother is genuinely interested in people. It's a beautiful quality, rather rare, but I'd say it was quite a different matter from suing for the acquaintance of people for no other reason than not to find yourself arrived at Saturday night *uninvited.*" Barbara had not looked satisfied, so he'd continued. "The plumber comes here to repair the sink, and before he leaves he and your mother have discussed amateur bird-watching with a good deal of pleasure and enthusiasm. She doesn't say to him, What are your hobbies, sir? It simply emerges, as he tinkers with the sink, that the plumber likes bird-watching. She comes to have lunch with me at the school, and in fifteen minutes Dr. Paley is telling her how bitterly his son hates Alaska. I didn't know his son hated Alaska. In fact, I'm not sure I knew he had a son. But does all this mean that then we're to start exchanging dinners with the plumber and Dr. Paley? Of course not. They don't want it, and neither does she. She's just the sort of person who goes through life enriching *any* contact. But you can't judge most of us by her. You can't even theorize much about her. Pure theory can never banish wonder. And the person of true empathy is a wonder, and your mother's a person of true empathy."

"That's a nice line," Barbara had said, impressed if not convinced. "About pure theory and wonder."

"William James," he conceded.

Now she stood, half-attending to Peter's explanation

to Max of how he had glasses for driving, in the glove compartment of the car, but didn't want to wear them to the party as they didn't match his tie . . . it seemed to be something like that he was saying . . . half-remembering her father's words. Is he right? she thought. It would be such a relief, to be able to believe him, to be able to stop fretting about what people thought of you, said of you, to stop worrying about what you'd said last week, yesterday, how you'd sounded on the phone, to stop agreeing with everybody in order to sound agreeable. To stop, in other words, wanting everyone to like you, when it was clearly impossible, probably not desirable, and so far had only resulted in making you dislike yourself far too often. Was he right? And—she made a note to ask him this sometime—had he been so independent when *he* was fifteen?

He'd been trying to help her. In this, as in so many of the things he said, he was trying to have her benefit from his experience. But could a girl of fifteen benefit from the experience of a man of forty? Maybe a little, she admitted. Maybe, if you listened and were willing, you could take to yourself a small part of his experience and be better for it. But I'll bet when he was fifteen he wanted people to like him. Not as much as I do (but then, I carry everything to extremes, she told herself a little proudly), but he was not indifferent. And I wouldn't believe him if he told me that he was. People that age forget.

Margaret was beside her, saying in her slightly husky voice, "How're you, Barby? I'm so glad you could come."

Barbara looked at her, at the short springy hair, the direct bright eyes, the fine bones and animated posture. Margaret had always given her the impression that she could, if she wished, merely leave the floor and sail from one point to another. She listened to the throaty, friendly voice, and the tension within her loosened. She could almost feel it flowing away through her fingertips, as she said, "I'm glad, too." Did she dare to call her Margy? "Margy."

"Randy tells me he spent the whole afternoon playing in the snow with you and your brothers. What's the oldest one's name? Andrew. He's divine."

Barbara blinked. "How did you know him?"

"Oh, he comes over now and then to play with my kid brother. Though, to tell the truth, he's the devil and all to snag. Rob always behaves like he's bagged a . . . a phoenix, or something, when he gets Andrew over here. You must have met Rob at your house? He's been there with Andrew a few times."

"No. Yes. I mean, of course I've met him. But you know, there are so many children—" Feeble, false. Andrew did not bring so many children home that she could not have gotten their names. Probably he'd just said, "This is Rob." If he'd said Rob Obemeyer . . . Realizing where this line of thinking was taking her, Barbara dropped it hastily, guiltily. I just don't pay attention to people, she said to herself harshly. This was kinder than admitting she'd have paid attention if the name had been right.

I am not a nice person. No, not a nice person at all. So how had this miracle happened? How was it that she stood now, a guest, an apparently quite welcome guest, of Margaret Obemeyer's, whom she'd envied and wished to know for so long? Well, it was nothing she could ask. Probably better never to find out. It had happened, and now, please God, she would make the most of her opportunity.

"I love this room," she said. Oh, *ruin*. She had already *said* that.

But Margaret seemed pleased. "You must be sure to tell Mother. She and Dad will be down in a while. Mom's as proud of this room as a peacock." She was suddenly amused. "Mom really has a time of it, because she can't like anything that six other people have heard of. So the house is forever being changed. But do tell her—" She broke off as the front bell rang, her head lifting happily. "Excuse me, Barbara. The door." She fairly flew to open it, and there was Bud Parker, stamping snow off his boots in the vestibule.

CHAPTER SIX

It seemed that for Margaret, therefore automatically for the rest of them, the party began with Bud's arrival. Mr. and Mrs. Obemeyer came downstairs at that moment, as if on cue, entered the living room and held brief court. They did not emphasize, but managed to convey, the fact that their presence was assured for the evening. We won't be seen but we'll be here, were their unsaid words.

They were extremely gracious. A stout, comfortable couple who seemed to Barbara far older than her own parents. They probably weren't, but they had a settled, substantial way about them, as though all the important questions had been satisfactorily answered, and they did not propose to inquire further into anything. Mrs. Obemeyer might change her household décor all the time, but she seemed herself unchangeable, and so did her husband beside her. It gave them an old air.

When they got to Barbara (or she to them, this was organized almost like a receiving line), she said, "My mother said to give you her remembrances."

"Ah, yes," said Mrs. Obemeyer, "and mine, please, to her. Do you know Mrs. Perry, Jim? No? A lovely person. Like quicksilver." She looked at Barbara. "I say this to her face, mind. Just like quicksilver." Barbara began to remark that it was a very nice thing to say to someone's face, then realized that in Mrs. Obemeyer's philosophy this might be doubtful. She smiled. "Yes, a lovely person," Mrs. Obemeyer repeated, as if to erase the quicksilver metaphor. "And so willing to believe the best of everyone." Again she looked as if she'd said something not wholly agreeable. "Do give her my regards," she said hastily, but with warmth, and handed Barbara back to the party, as it were.

There was a fire in the game room, too. A big fire in a big hearth, above which a big head of a grizzly bear grinned dismally. (Barbara saw why Andrew wouldn't come here often. There were several other heads, deer, mostly, on the pine-paneled walls, and a tiger skin on the floor. No, Andrew would not like it here.) A ping-pong table at one end of the room didn't crowd it at all. There was a good-sized bar, with ice buckets and soft drinks, bowls of peanuts and popcorn ranged along the top. A half-dozen chrome and red leather bar stools stood against it. There was a phonograph, an upright piano. The cork floors were glossy and at one side had an inset shuffleboard arrangement. The walls, in addition to decapitated animals, had wooden shields with mottoes on them ("The opinions of the husband in this household are not necessarily those of the management," "Think or thwim," "Don't go away mad—just go away"), and a shelf that ran at head height along one wall and held at least a hundred different kinds of beer steins. Bamboo blinds, splattered with primary colors, stood in stiff folds at the windows. This place might be on a subterranean floor, but it could never be referred to as anything other than the game room.

Margaret and Randy began piling records on the phonograph, while Max, Pete, Alice and Sonia converged on the ping-pong table. Bud and Jeff stood turning their hands before the fire, Jeff talking away indefatigably, Bud smiling his shy, slow smile. He looked over at Barbara, made a move as though to approach her, was detained by Jeff's voice.

"Want a Coke?" said Connie Frost, tripping to her side. "Honestly, talking with Mrs. Obemeyer makes me so *thursday.*"

Thursday? thought Barbara. Oh, yes. Baby talk. She followed Connie to the bar, and they perched on the chrome stools, Connie chattering in her high, light voice. "Notice how she made it clear they'd be around, without *akshally* saying it? The Obemeyers never leave the house when Margy's giving a do. Neither do my folks. Any more."

"Any more?"

"Last summer I gave a watermelon party, and Mummy and Daddy went out, and the boys were *awful*. They threw watermelon all over the place, and one of them broke a lamp, and honest*ly*, it was practically juvenile delinquency. We were furious. The girls, I mean. Mostly because we had to clean it all up the next day. We were having a slumber party afterward, you see, and the boys left fairly early, but not before they'd made a mess of everything, *in*cluding themselves." She twirled a straw in her glass, poked her finger at the ice, made a little face at Barbara.

"These same boys?" Barbara asked incredulously, but part of her took time to think of the slumber parties, the watermelon parties, the many parties that had gone on all these years, that she had never got to, and had only known of accidentally, through talk around the school. Well, I'm here now, she scolded herself. Stop thinking of what's *past*—

Connie was looking around the room. "Except Bud and Pete. Savages, that's what they were. They've been better since then, by golly. My father made every one of them come over to the house the next day and he talked to them. When my father talks to people, they don't think they've been whispered at," she said gravely. "I was sort of sorry for Randy, but the rest of them deserved it."

"Why Randy, especially?" Did her voice catch when she mentioned his name? He was over there, laughing with Margaret. He looked so blond, so strong, so . . . engaging. This afternoon I was in love with him. And now? She turned abruptly to Connie, wanting to hear more about him.

"Well, Randy didn't really join in the melee, because he knew what he'd catch from his father if he did, so then he caught it from my father, anyway. But he didn't say anything. Mum's the word, and don't rat on the gang, and all that sort of mush that boys say they believe in. They're half brothers, you know. I mean, my father and Randy's. Uncle George. He's stricter than Daddy, and Daddy after all does have his soft side. Mummy says it's because they're both so highly principled, that's why they terrify people, but Daddy's not nearly as bad, and at least he *talks* once in a while. When Mummy and I will let him, that is," she giggled. "Mummy and I are *dedicated* to talking. Does this bore you?"

"Not at all," Barbara said, with complete sincerity.

"Well, and so . . . What was my point?" She didn't wait for clarification. Apparently if she lost one point, she found dozens of others to light on. "And Aunt Marian—she's Randy's mother—is just sort of, sort of *defeated* by all this, and who wouldn't be, living with a man with all those principles and not talking *either*, and I'll bet *days* go by in that house when they don't even say boo to each other, and I don't think I could stand it," she mused. "How did you happen to come tonight? Not that I don't think it's lovely and all, and we did have fun caroling the other night, didn't we? But I just wondered."

She sure carries the little-girl role right through to the end, Barbara thought. But, oddly, the question from Connie did not disturb her. She seemed so completely without malice. Barbara remembered that Katy referred to her as an "itty-bitty blonde." "Into everyone's life," Katy had said, "an itty-bitty blonde must fall, and the only thing to do is wait and hope it will go away." Her implication had been that itty-bitty blondes were also stupid. But I don't know, Barbara thought now. I don't think Connie's stupid. Sort of loose-tongued, maybe. I'll bet she gets her father wild at times. And her mother, who is so much like her, probably does, too. And I'll bet neither one of them pays a bit of attention, and after a while he just laughs and pats them on their itty-bitty blond heads and loves them.

"I don't know how she happened to," she said slowly. "But I'm glad." It was an easy thing to say, besides a true one. She didn't feel the least bit defensive with Connie, as she did with Sonia and Alice Ordway (who hadn't even spoken to her this evening), or suspicious, as she did with Max and Jeff.

"Oh, I'm glad, too," Connie said, reaching across her for some popcorn. "Don't misunderstand me. I'm curious as a cat, you know. Daddy says it's going to kill him, my curiosity, I mean. I guess because she asked Bud, and needed an extra girl. She only practically met him last night, you know, when he took her to the movies (because I was too much of a snob to go with him, Barbara thought), but I think she likes him *quite* a lot, and I must say he *is* a sort of dream, isn't he?"

Barbara, who hadn't thought so, glanced over at Bud, and saw that he was, indeed, a sort of dream. Slender, diffident, with quiet dark features and a quick suffusing smile.

"Not my type," Connie was going on, her glance moving to Jeff's big form. She sighed. "No question of it . . . the bigger they are, the harder I fall. Once last fall he sort of got interested in Alice." (You had to understand her pronouns from the context of her talk, since she didn't trouble to sort them out.) She looked, a little frown appearing on her forehead, in the direction of the ping-pong game, proceeding noisily and gaily at the far end of the room. Alice, flicking her racket with strong wrist motions, had Max beside himself trying to return her shots. The other two were watching. Through the music from the gramophone, the roar of the fire, came the delicate sound of the ping-pong ball striking racket, table, racket. It isn't, Barbara thought, like any other sound in the world. She looked at Alice, moving gracefully and firmly, her skirts swinging. She had a full, sullen mouth and a great deal of curly chestnut hair held back with combs and pins. She reached up to adjust a comb as she returned one of Max's serves, and he yelped with fury.

"Did you . . . mind?" Barbara asked. Connie seemed to invite personal questions, and didn't take offense when they were asked.

"Mind?" she squealed. "I thought I was dying, and I could hardly wait. Never have I been treated so ignonomously."

"Ignominiously," Jeff said, coming up beside her, and putting a hand on her shoulder. "Who's been treating you ignominiously?"

Connie tipped her head up to him. "Not ignonomously?" she said. "Dear, dear . . . that's the way I've been saying it all my life. I *hope* I haven't said it in front of anybody important." She leaped down from the bar stool. "Let's dance, Jeff." She held up her arms, her little figure close to his, and they moved off to the music, both of them talking. Pete and Sonia left the vicinity of the ping-pong table, and began a sinuous, sedate version of the jitterbugging that fascinated Barbara, who was a good dancer herself. But they're . . . terrific, she thought, watching so intently that Randy had to tap her lightly on the shoulder to indicate his presence.

"Dance?"

"Oh, I'd love to."

Randy had the freshest, cleanest smell, very faintly redolent of some masculine after-shave lotion, although —gently, as if by accident, she rubbed her cheek against his—although he didn't, obviously, shave yet. He was a lithe, inventive dancer. It was funny, how different boys danced. Some of them holding you much too tightly—not because you were you, but because they just naturally held any girl too tightly—and somehow getting in your way, so that you were far too aware of them (not happily) and in some fashion cut off from the music; some of them keeping you at a distance, so concentrated on their own feet and what to do with them that you felt completely extraneous; some of them clutching you loosely, their fingers bunching your dress in the back, giving you a puppet-like sensation. And some of them danced like Randy—though none, she decided, as well—holding you lightly, firmly, as though they were glad to be dancing, and glad that it was with you. The good dancers always gave you that feeling, though at Fortnightlies or church dances, they left you very readily when the dance was finished. At least, she amended, they've always left me willingly enough. She realized this without a trace of self-pity, wondered why, and looked up to find Randy's blue eyes fixed on hers. It's because I feel safe. I can say a thing like that to myself because Randy isn't going to leave me alone against the wall, wondering where the next dance is coming from.

"That was fun, this afternoon," he said.

"It was. Lots of fun," she said softly, quite forgetting her rage and hurt, her sense of exclusion, her outburst of fury toward her parents and her brothers. It had been fun. It had been a lovely afternoon of snow and laughter, cocoa and conversation, an afternoon of change, and newness, and going forward.

"I think your family is great," he said. She accepted this gravely, pleasurably, with understanding. She felt a sudden yearning sense of pity and love (not the being *in* love response, though she thought that would come again) for this boy, who lived in a house where people had principles but no warmth, perpetuating for himself family sayings from his childhood and trying to share them with others. Her eyes blurred a little with gratitude that she and her family had something real to offer him, and had somehow been given a chance to offer it.

"I hope you come and see us again," she said. "I mean, a lot."

"Oh, don't worry," he said with a smile. "I intend to."

They laughed, a ringing young laugh that was filled with so much joy that the others turned their heads to see. And Barbara, whirling in the middle of this group, this Nortown, Ohio, clique, looked at them. At Sonia and Alice, who did not especially like her (but who might, in time, and did it really matter if they did not?), at Max and Pete, whom she scarcely knew (but might, sometime), at Margaret and Connie and Bud, who did like her (it was not a thing she had to question and tear apart and brood over). Then she looked back to Randy, and his arm tightened around her just a little.

They danced.

Set in Linotype Baskerville
Manufactured by The Haddon Craftsmen, Inc.
Published by HARPER & BROTHERS, *New York*